# LAUREN CANAN

—

# MARRIAGE AT ANY PRICE

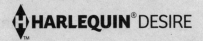

Recycling programs
for this product may
not exist in your area.

ISBN-13: 978-1-335-60362-3

Marriage at Any Price

Copyright © 2019 by Sarah Cannon

Printed in U.S.A.

When **Lauren Canan** began writing, stories of romance and unbridled passion flowed through her fingers onto the page. Today she is a multi-award-winning author, including the prestigious Romance Writers of America Golden Heart® Award. She lives in Texas with her own real-life hero, two chaotic dogs and a mouthy parrot named Bird. Find her on Facebook or visit her website, laurencanan.com.

## Books by Lauren Canan

### Harlequin Desire

*Terms of a Texas Marriage*
*Lone Star Baby Bombshell*

### The Masters of Texas

*Redeeming the Billionaire SEAL*
*One Night with the Texan*
*Stranger in His Bed*
*Marriage at Any Price*

Visit her Author Profile page at Harlequin.com, or laurencanan.com, for more titles.

You can find Lauren Canan on Facebook, along with other Harlequin Desire authors, at Facebook.com/harlequindesireauthors!

# One

It all happened in the blink of an eye.

There was a blur of motion to Seth Masters's right as a woman on a large thoroughbred came out of nowhere. She gave a cue, and the immense muscles in the animal's hind legs propelled the steed and its rider up and over the hood of Seth's low-slung sports car. He fought to bring the car to a screeching halt, narrowly missing one of the pines that grew on both sides of the country road. The rider stopped as well, turned the chestnut around and headed back to the car. She didn't look happy.

"You're an idiot!" she said as she brought the horse to a stop a few feet from the car. "Didn't you see the signs saying Slow Down, Bridle Path Ahead?

Can't you read? You almost got us killed! Who goes eighty on a one-lane backwoods road?"

"I wasn't going eighty."

"Couldn't prove it by me!"

Seth was flooded with emotions: shock, relief that no one was hurt, an underlying sense of unease that he'd been driving too fast. But through all the self-recrimination, one thought stood out: the woman was magnificent. Rich auburn hair swirled about her almost angelic face, and though her green eyes sparkled with anger, they were stunning. Her slim, beautiful body seemed too slight to control the huge thoroughbred that tossed his head and pawed the ground, pulling air into its massive lungs. Obviously she was an expert rider, something Seth was enormously grateful for right now.

He opened the door and pushed out of the Ferrari. What could he say? He'd been so wrapped up in his own thoughts he hadn't paid any attention to the signs.

"I apologize. Sincerely. I hope you weren't hurt."

"Just slow down. The riding path crisscrosses the road several times over the next few miles. Needless to say, the next time you might not be so lucky."

Even in anger her voice was clear and attractive.

"Point taken."

She homed in on his face and tipped her head as a frown crossed her fine features.

"You're not from around here." It was a statement as much as a question.

"Los Angeles."

She opened her mouth as if she was about to say something else then must have thought better of it and shook her head.

"Could you tell me how far out I am from Calico Springs?"

"By the posted speed limit, about twenty minutes."

"Thanks," he replied, taking in her sexy-as-hell physique as she turned the stallion around and headed back in the direction they'd come, disappearing into the trees.

Seth returned to the car and started the engine. He hoped this wasn't a sign of what was in store this trip. He had to remember this wasn't LA—it was rural Texas, and things worked at a slower pace. Still not able to completely shake off the close encounter, he eased back out onto the narrow road and continued in the direction of Calico Springs.

Attorney Ben Rucker's office, an old Victorian house just off the town square, was easy to spot. It fit in perfectly with the other buildings along Main Street. Calico Springs was quaint. Innocent. Like a town out of the past. There were planters filled with flowers and wooden park benches in front of most of the stores and shops. After parking the car, he made his way inside the lawyer's air-conditioned office and gave his name to the receptionist.

"Of course, Mr. Masters. Mr. Rucker has been expecting you. I'll let him know you're here."

Minutes later Seth was seated across from the elderly attorney.

"It's a pleasure to meet you, Mr. Masters. I take it this is the first time you've been to Calico Springs?"

"Actually, I've been here several times. I met my half brothers and enjoyed the area when I was a young boy. I've been back a dozen or so times since then. The last time was about five years ago."

The attorney chuckled. "You certainly carry the family resemblance. You are most definitely a Masters."

"I wanted to come down early and see the ranch again. Do my brothers know I'm here?"

"I told them you were coming. Chance and Cole are in New York, and Wade and his wife are in London. They will all be back next week for the probate of the will."

Seth nodded. He'd been brought up the only child of a single mother. Then when he was six years old, his father had insisted he come to the ranch and meet his half brothers. Even at that age, he'd been nervous. But they had taken the news of his existence better than he'd hoped and welcomed him into the family. Those dozen or so summers he'd spent on the ranch were wonderful memories, and he looked forward to seeing everyone again.

"I must admit I'm curious about the will."

"I can understand." Mr. Rucker sat back in his leather chair. "Did you know your father very well?"

Seth shrugged. "About as much as anyone knew him, I guess. I saw him maybe a dozen times in my life. Mother wouldn't talk about him. I never saw or heard from him again after I entered Stanford, al-

LAUREN CANAN 11

though I always suspected there was communication between him and my mother."

As he'd grown older, Seth had begun to realize that the home where he and his mother lived and the cars she drove were beyond the means of a single working mother who had no advanced degree. There had to be another source of funds. And though he'd been awarded a partial scholarship to attend Stanford, it hadn't nearly covered all the expenses. Yet when he needed money, it was always provided.

"From what little I know," Mr. Rucker said, "you would be right. Your father spoke highly of you when we were drafting the will. But he was never a man comfortable with family. Either of his families, as it turns out. His work always took priority. I guess he had his own reasons why he couldn't relate."

"I guess." Seth nodded. "The reason I mention the will is I sit on the boards of two regional hospitals, and a new research facility focusing on leukemia is on the table. The more funding we can get for it, the better. If I stand to inherit anything, it will certainly help me move things along."

The attorney nodded then seemed to hesitate. "Mr. Masters, you understand I cannot discuss the will without all heirs being present. But that said, I feel it only fair to ask if you're married."

"Married?" The question seemed odd. He'd come close once. It had ended badly. He'd given his heart to Gwen Jeffers, and she'd returned his love by having an affair with another man. He hadn't thought of getting married to anyone since. He liked life in the fast lane. Free of responsibility to anyone but himself and his companies. "No," he replied. "Not me. Why do you ask?"

"Well, there's a stipulation that needs to be met by the time we're in probate, so I'd better discuss this with you. One of the requirements of the will is that each of you boys be married. Mr. Masters never explained his reasoning. It may have had something to do with his own experiences in life. I'll never know for sure. But, of course, he had the right to set any conditions he wanted. If any of you aren't married by the day the will is probated, you'll be dropped from the will, and any financial assets or land holdings will revert to the other married sons or, in specific circumstances, to charity. As of now, you're the only one who doesn't meet the requirement.

"I tried to call to discuss this with you a few weeks ago, but you were out of the country. I left several messages with your office. I asked your brothers if they knew your marital status, but they couldn't say for sure—apparently you haven't been in touch recently."

"I see. Yeah, I have a boatload of calls I need to return. I regret not getting in touch sooner. This news is disappointing." And that was an understatement. "But—it is what it is. I look forward to seeing my brothers again and meeting their wives. It isn't every day I get to spend time with them."

"That's true." The lawyer chuckled. "It's too bad about the will. It sounds like the research center is a worthy cause."

"It is." Seth stood up from his chair and shook the lawyer's hand. "Well, thank you, Mr. Rucker. I appreciate you letting me know."

"Of course, Mr. Masters. You do have ten days or so. Perhaps you know someone who'd consider becoming your wife. There's still time."

"I don't think so, but again, thanks."

Seth stepped out of the lawyer's office with Mr. Rucker close behind him just as the front door opened and in walked none other than the horsewoman he'd met on the road. Her surprise at seeing Seth was immediate. But she quickly put it aside and turned toward Mr. Rucker.

"Did you get an appointment?"

"Ally, why don't you come back after lunch and we can discuss it in private."

"I have to go back to work. All I'm asking for is a yes or no."

"I'm sorry." He smiled at her and slowly shook his head. "I'm trying to get in touch with Wade or Cole, since they handle the company's finances. Wade is out of the country. Cole and Chance are in New York doing double duty while their brother is gone. Why don't we step inside my office for a moment?"

"I don't have time," she insisted. "You will excuse us, won't you?" she said looking at Seth, then turned back to Mr. Rucker.

The elderly gentleman held up his hands to Seth in a gesture of helplessness.

"It's okay," Seth said, grinning. "I'll be going."

"I managed to speak with Chance," Mr. Rucker

said to the young woman, "and he said he knew nothing about it and we would have to wait until Wade returned."

"And when will that be?"

"When his business is finished, I gather. I believe he has an appointment here in the latter part of next week."

Seth heard her sigh behind him. Whatever they were talking about appeared to do nothing to improve her state of obvious frustration. She must be having a really bad day.

Still, Seth couldn't help but catch the names Mr. Rucker had tossed out. Wade, Cole and Chance were his half brothers. He was tempted to blurt out his relationship and see if he could help her but at the last second closed his mouth. It wasn't any of his business.

"Can you schedule an appointment for me then?"

"I'll see what I can do, Ally. You know I will, but…"

"You think it's pointless," she finished.

"I think," the attorney said, "that you have every right to talk with them. And to that end, I'll do the best I can."

"Thanks, Mr. Rucker."

As she turned to leave, her emerald eyes fell on Seth.

"I see you made it to town, presumably without mowing anyone else down."

"Miracles do happen. Actually, I did slow down

after our encounter and enjoyed the countryside," Seth said. "Thanks for the tip."

"Any time."

He opened the door and she walked through it, turning right and continuing down the sidewalk. Seth couldn't help but watch as she seemed to glide down the street. She was still wearing the riding pants that outlined every detail of her slim figure. A leather belt emphasized her tiny waist, and her loose white shirt covered full breasts. She had a small, impish nose and lips a man could enjoy for hours. He felt his body immediately react to her, something that frankly surprised him.

It was too bad he didn't pick up any vibes that she was the marrying kind. He just might be tempted.

"Mr. Rucker, could you recommend a good place to eat?" Seth said, turning back to look at the lawyer.

"Burdall's City Café, just one block up on the town square. As a matter of fact, I was about to head there myself. You're welcome to share my table."

"Thanks. I'd like that."

It was only a few minutes' walk to the café, and they just beat the lunchtime rush. Seth pulled out a chair and settled in across the table from Mr. Rucker. He grabbed the menu from between the salt, pepper and sugar canisters and looked it over. It had a pretty wide selection for a small hometown restaurant.

A waitress set tall glasses of ice water down next to them and said she'd be back in just a few minutes to take their orders. But before she could return, they had another visitor at their table.

"Hi." It was the redhead again. "Do you mind if I join you? There's a line and I have to get back to work."

"Of course," said Mr. Rucker without hesitation. "Ally, have you met Mr. Masters?"

She stilled. "No," she said, staring at Seth. "Not… formally, at least."

"This is Seth Masters. Seth, Ally Kincaid."

"Masters?" She frowned. Her eyes narrowed. "Are you any relation to Wade Masters?"

"Yes. As a matter of fact I am."

"I knew it. When you almost ran me down on the road. You look like a Masters." Her eyes rested on him, and she was silent for a few moments. Then, as though she thought better of saying what she had in mind, she changed the subject.

"You said you were from California, right? What do you do there?" she asked as she pulled out a chair and sat down.

"I own several companies, mostly electronics and pharmaceuticals."

"Huh. Who would have thought? I would have better believed you were a contender for the Indianapolis 500." She reached for a menu. "I'll bet your pharmacy comes in handy when you get behind the wheel."

"I'm just used to moving at a faster pace."

"Yeah, I'll bet you are. So, what are you doing in the sleepy little town of Calico Springs?"

"Just enjoying the view," he replied, looking straight at her.

Seth watched as a light blush ran up her neck and touched her face before he returned to the menu. Her very scent was exciting: a subtle blend of exotic herbs, strawberries and leather. It had his pheromones working overtime. He had never experienced such an immediate attraction to a woman.

"Is everyone ready to order?" The waitress flipped a page in her notebook and took pen in hand.

Ally ordered a ham and cheese sandwich while Mr. Rucker and Seth chose to have steak. Seth glanced at the older man and saw a twinkle in his eyes. He suspected Ben was attuned to the banter going on between him and Ally and maybe had a little subtle matchmaking in mind.

After they had given their orders Ally turned her focus to Mr. Rucker. "So, did you pencil me in?"

"I had my secretary send Wade a text to see when he's available. Once I hear back, consider yourself penciled."

"Good. Thank you. I just hope he's as reasonable as people say he is."

She wanted an appointment with Wade? Seth couldn't help but wonder as to the reason.

As though the question showed on his face, she set the menu aside and said flatly, "Wade Masters's father stole my ranch. And I want it back."

# Two

"Ally," Mr. Rucker said in a cautioning tone, indicating she had spoken out of turn.

"What?" She shrugged her shoulders. "I don't care who hears. Half the town knows anyway." She turned her focus on the newcomer. "The old man was a crook. He stole my ranch. Claimed my father used it for a loan that Dad never paid back. My father wouldn't do something like that. Old man Masters took it all. Everything. Had me evicted after Dad died. I even had to fight to keep three mares and a stallion that were registered in *my* name. Talk about greed. You'd think someone with that much money wouldn't feel the need to swindle people out of their home."

"The horses, as I recall, were simply a misunderstanding," Mr. Rucker asserted.

"Yeah. How long would it have taken to straighten that out had I not caught it?"

When Ally turned away from Seth Masters, she could still feel his golden eyes watching her. Ben Rucker was probably right. She shouldn't be spouting off in front of strangers, although she found it hard to consider Seth Masters a stranger. He could almost be Wade Masters's brother, so alike were their looks. He had thick brown hair with a slight wave and gold highlights and a five o'clock shadow that covered a sharp jaw and prominent chin, complete with a sexy little cleft. High cheekbones complimented brown eyes with flecks of gold. His lips, too kissable to put into words, delivered a sexy grin showing perfect white teeth. In his white dress shirt and tie, he was the epitome of handsome.

"What about you, Ally? What do you do?" he asked.

"Rancher. Or I used to be before…" She grimaced and pressed her lips together. "Now I work at the Triple Bar Ranch east of town. I train horses."

"That must take a lot of skill and agility."

She'd never really thought about it. It was something she'd done most of her life. She shrugged. "Maybe."

The man nodded. "I would venture to say our jobs are equally challenging."

"Oh, you would, huh? Tell me, Mr. Masters, how many stalls have you mucked out? How many horses have you trained?" She couldn't help but laugh. The idea that she was anything like this rich hunk from California was absurd.

Ben Rucker snorted at her comment and fought not to choke on his coffee.

"It just so happens," Seth said, "that in my younger days, I mucked out plenty of stalls. Never trained a new horse, but logged plenty of hours exercising them. I spent most summers here in Calico Springs at the family ranch growing up. So I guess I have a good idea of what you do. Clearly you're accomplished. And that's worth saying."

"Thank you," she replied, feeling a blush coming on. "Still…my accomplishments probably don't measure up compared to yours."

"You don't accept compliments very well, do you?"

"Compliments I can handle. It's bullshit I'm not so good with."

"Then allow me to backtrack and just say you're a very skilled horsewoman."

"Damn good thing for you." She sat back as the waitress set her plate down in front of her. "It took me most of the ride back to the ranch to calm Monkey down."

"What happened to Monkey?" Ben asked.

"He had a fright this morning," she said, picking up half of her sandwich. "Some idiot nearly ran him down with his car."

"Good grief!"

"No grief. Just bad driving." She took a bite and picked up a napkin.

"Not that bad or I would have hit you. And it occurs to me that I wasn't the only one speeding."

"I take it you two have met each other before, then?" asked Ben.

"We almost had a collision on the country road leading to town this morning," Seth explained.

Ally dropped the sandwich back onto her plate, wiped her hands with the paper napkin and glared at him. "There's no speed limit posted on the bridle path. Most people with any common sense would appreciate the fact that it's the cars going down the road that are the hazard. Especially if they are trying to break the sound barrier."

"I say again, I was not going all that fast."

"That would depend on your definition of fast."

They held each other's gaze. After a few long seconds, she turned back to her plate. "You were in the wrong, and I really don't care to discuss it further."

She couldn't miss his pursed lips as he tried to hide a grin.

Hateful man. She didn't know what he was doing in Calico Springs. She hadn't missed how he'd sidestepped her question when she asked. And she hadn't appreciated that "enjoying the view" remark, even though it had been a long time since a man flirted with her. She didn't want any of the Masters men to say one word to her after what their father had done. She could only hope their paths would not cross again.

* * *

"I ordered fifty sacks of sweet feed and one hundred and twenty-five sacks of Nature's Best. What out of that says crimped oats? Does Colby have a hearing disorder now?"

She'd stopped by the feed store on her way home to pick up the order for the horses she was training. Instead of what she ordered, they had readied seventy-five sacks of oats. This day just seemed to keep going downhill.

"I'm sorry, Ally. If you can give me a few minutes, I'll fix your order. Are you in the farm truck?"

"Yeah. Thanks. I'll wait outside."

Despite the obstacles she'd overcome so far today, mostly set in her path by that Seth Masters, it was still a beautiful day with just enough fluffy white clouds overhead to keep the sun from turning up the heat. She wandered out to the gardening section and idly looked at the petunias and other bedding plants. Any other year, she would be picking up trays of assorted flowers to be planted in the beds around the large wraparound porch at her house. This year she had purchased one hanging basket that she placed at the edge of the small front porch of the cabin where she stayed, and that was all she would allow herself to have. No use spending money on stuff that would just die from neglect.

And they would be neglected. Her heart just wasn't in it. The cabin, provided by the ranch where she worked, sufficed, but it wasn't home. It would never be home. Why surround herself with tarnished memories of the things she used to love? She didn't need to be reminded of her home and the joy she'd known there. It was gone, and the sooner she accepted that fact, the better off she would be.

She would keep the appointment with Wade Masters once it was arranged, but down deep she knew she had little hope of convincing him to give back her ranch. Even if he agreed to sell it back to her, she didn't make enough money for monthly payments on a ranch that size. It would take time, at least another year, before she could start earning the kind of money she needed.

"It seems we keep bumping into each other." A deep voice came from behind her. Before she fully turned toward him, she knew it was Seth Masters.

"Are you following me, Masters?"

"On the contrary, I've been around back looking at the tractors. I didn't see you when I got here, so I would have to ask you the same question."

He smiled. She gritted her teeth and glared.

"So what are you going to do with a tractor?"

"Someday I might buy some land. And I've always been fascinated with tractors. The bedding plants look rich and healthy," he added, filling the intervals when she didn't respond. "Are you doing your flower beds in these?"

"I have no land. I have no house. Consequently, I have no flower beds. So no, I'm not buying any plants."

"I saw this store and had to stop. You don't often see old businesses like this still open and running.

Most have been replaced by the newer franchises." He looked around at the large assortment of plants, hanging baskets and trees. "It's things like the old wood-burning stove inside and the sign on the back door. Have you seen it? 'This store is guarded by a double-barrel shotgun two nights a week. Pick your night.' You just don't find that kind of thing in the city. I think it's charming."

*Charming?* "You're kidding."

"No, not at all."

"How long are you in town?" She couldn't keep herself from asking. If he would be in and around the area, she needed to know it and be prepared for any more chance encounters.

"Just a few weeks this trip. I've been considering buying a small place with some land and a barn. I've always loved horses. Ridden most of my life." He shrugged. "This might be a great location."

"It's a little far from LA."

"Just a couple of hours by plane."

"It is a nice area. I'll give you that. And *most* of the people are friendly and aboveboard."

"Hey, Ally." She turned to see two feed store employees walking toward her, their shoulders laden with sacks of grain. "You in that black truck? We got your feed."

"Yeah. Make sure you have the right order this time."

"Yep. We got it. No crimped oats this trip?"

"That would be correct. Oh. Could you throw in two large mineral blocks, Jack?" She considered her mental list for a brief second to see if she could re-member anything else she needed. "I think that will do it."

Soon the correct bags of feed and two mineral blocks were loaded into the back of the truck. As she walked to the driver's side, she again heard some-one call her name.

"Ms. Kincaid?" Seth Masters stood at the back of the truck. "Would you like to have dinner with me tonight?"

The question was so unexpected, it took her a few seconds to realize he was waiting for an answer. "Ah…actually, I have prior commitments. I hope you find your tractor and whatever else you need."

She wasn't used to lying. It made her feel horrible. She didn't trust the man, but he hadn't really done anything to her—other than almost run her down. He was here alone and probably just wanted a little company. Still…he was a Masters.

"Thanks. I think I have. Well, good to see you again."

"Yeah," she mumbled as she climbed into the driver's seat and started the truck. The day did not exist that she would have dinner with a Masters. To-day's lunch had been bad enough. Then, she hadn't known who he was. He may or may not be closely in-volved with the clan of thieves who'd stolen her fam-ily's land, but she wasn't about to take the chance. He'd said he was related. From his apparent age, and given that he looked exactly like Wade Masters, he could very well be their brother. But he hadn't grown up around here, otherwise she would have heard of him before. It made her wonder what he was up to.

As she backed out and headed for the main road, she noticed him still standing next to the fertilizer. He looked up and nodded as she passed. He seemed nice enough, but there was still the question of why he was here. Calico Springs was barely a dot on the map. It certainly wasn't the vacation capital of the world. Probably he was here visiting his family. But they were all out of town, according to Mr. Rucker. While it was none of her business, overall it was a bit suspicious. She didn't like suspicious. Especially when it involved the name Masters.

Seth decided time was on his side to do some house hunting. It was just over a week until his brothers were due back, according to Ben Rucker. It would give him a chance to find a local place to call home; he already had penthouses dotted around the US and the UK. Now that his business was well enough established that he could take some time off on occasion, having property in this area would afford him the chance to see more of his family.

"We have several ranches that fit your description, Mr. Masters. Shall we plan on a time to go and see a few of them?"

Seth sat across the desk from Kathy Chisum, the broker for Chisum Real Estate. Ben Rucker had recommended her as one of the better agents in the county representing the largest number of farms and ranches. He figured while he waited for Wade,

Chance and Cole to return, he might as well look at some properties. He hadn't been lying when he'd told Ally Kincaid he was thinking of buying in this area. So far he liked what he'd seen. The quaint town sat in the center of rolling hills and far-reaching pastureland dotted with groves of pine and oak and a number of small lakes.

"That's fine. Any time. Any day," he replied. "I'll be here for a couple of weeks, and my schedule is pretty much open."

"What about right now? I've had a cancellation." Her voice was sweet and sincere.

"Works for me. Thanks, Ms. Chisum."

"Kathy." She smiled and rose from her chair. "Shall we take my truck?"

"Sure."

The first two properties they saw had most of the things he wanted in a ranch, but he found something wrong with both of them. He didn't want an old dairy farm. He didn't want a house with two bedrooms that would require major renovation. But the third ranch was almost perfect. White pipe fencing ran along both sides of the driveway. The house was a charmer. It was an example of antebellum architecture that was in remarkably good shape, although it could use a good paint job. Across the front and sides of the house, large white columns rose to the top of the second story, and a portico in the center drew the eye to the magnificent front door. Someone had cared a lot for the house and property. A deep porch surrounded the home on the first floor, and second-story balconies overlooked the pasture and hills on all four sides. Two chimneys peeked over the roof. Inside, a grand staircase led to the second floor, which contained four bedrooms and a larger room with a sitting area that he assumed was the master. The kitchen and baths had been completely remodeled with granite countertops that complemented the hardwood floors.

From the back porch, a path led to the barn. There were approximately twenty stalls, tack room, wash rack and a large open area where hay could be stored for the winter. The smell inside the wooden structure was amazing. He recognized alfalfa and the scent of leather. It brought Ally to mind.

"Kathy, would you happen to know who owns this farm?"

"Sure, let me look that up." She tapped something into her phone. "Oh, wait. It's owned by the Masters family." She stepped back and eyed him closely. "Any relation?"

"Yeah, as a matter of fact."

"Then you know they have a large ranching operation on the west side of town, just over ninety thousand acres. This was a repossession and doesn't border their property, so they put it up for sale. But I guess you knew that."

"No, actually, I didn't. I'm not involved with the family business."

"The price they're asking is really good for this area. Well below market value. We've had a lot of interest. It won't be on the market very long." She turned to look at him. "I guess you want something away from the family compound?"

He nodded. "Would you happen to know who owned it before them?"

"Mmm. I'm afraid I don't know any of the history for sure. I could try and find out for you if you like."

"No. That won't be necessary. I like this place. I should talk to my brothers about it."

"Sure. If you're seriously considering it, don't wait too long."

He nodded. "I understand."

"It's getting late. If you have no plans, would you like to have dinner?"

"I'd like that." He smiled.

Kathy was a pretty, shapely brunette who appeared to like what she saw in him, and it wouldn't hurt to have a friendly meal with her. The problem was, he already had his mind wrapped around a certain perky redhead. And he was positive this last ranch had been Ally's.

On the way back to town, while Kathy chatted away, an idea began to form. Ally wanted her home back. He needed a wife. They both had a chance to get what they wanted with no strings attached. The ranch's low list price was certainly worth it if it ensured he would be included in the will where billions were at stake.

It was a crazy idea. He smiled to himself at the thought of her reaction. He suspected only the name Masters had prevented her from accepting his dinner invitation earlier. Would she dare dance with the devil and say yes to marriage? Become Mrs. Seth Masters? On the irony scale, that had to take the cake.

It would have to be a real marriage. One on paper for a few months. With the proper prenup, it shouldn't be a problem. He had developed a knack for reading people, and Ally did not fit the particulars of a gold digger. She had given no sign of wanting to know him better. In fact, she seemed to hate him, as much as someone could hate a person they didn't know. But she'd also impressed him as an honest person who only wanted what, in her mind, she was entitled to: her ranch.

When Ally got home the next day, Seth was waiting for her on the tiny front porch of her small cabin. It hadn't been hard to find; in fact, Ben Rucker had told him where she lived and provided directions. Seth had also confirmed since yesterday that the ranch Kathy had shown him used to belong to Ally's family. He'd been right about that.

She looked exhausted, surprised and anything but happy to see him. Admittedly not a reaction he was accustomed to.

She pulled up next to the convertible and hopped out of her old truck. "Did you get lost?" she asked as she approached where he sat. "'Cause I can tell you this isn't where you want to be."

"It's exactly where I want to be," he said. "I wanted to talk to you."

"Talk? Talk about what?"

"I think I found a place I want. I would like you to go with me tomorrow and look at it." She sighed and resolutely shook her head, so he jumped in before she could say no. "Look, I know we got off to a bad start. But I really do need your expertise. I've ridden horses off and on most of my life. But I've never had a ranch. I don't know the first thing about stocking a barn for the winter, so I can't know if there is adequate space. I know nothing about the equipment required. You said you grew up in this environment. I'm asking you to help me decide if this is the place I want to invest in."

"Why don't you ask your relatives?"

"They're out of town."

"What about Ben?"

"Rucker? I have a feeling he knows about as much as I do with regards to ranching. No. I assure you, I need *you*. Frankly, you're the only one who fits the bill." An understatement.

She was quiet a long time. Then, "Where is this place?"

"West of town. I can't remember the road names, but I'm sure I can take us there."

In the dim glow from the lamppost next to the driveway, he saw her lower her head. Was she thinking about her former home? Should he have just told her his plan here and now? He'd given it serious thought last night and decided that she might be more tempted to say yes if she were at her home when he hit her up with the idea. He could now see that might be taking unfair advantage. He drew in a breath, intending to explain, when she raised her head and looked at him.

"I guess I can do it. I have to work three horses in the morning, but I can skip the ones scheduled in the afternoon. How about one o'clock?"

"One o'clock is perfect. I'll pick you up here tomorrow?"

"In that?" She nodded toward the pricey sports car. "I wish you had a truck."

"Maybe I'll get one after I find a ranch."

"You'd better hurry. That's a rental unless I miss my guess. You'll tear out the undercarriage driving these rocky roads, not to mention the damage they will cause to the body and the paint job. You'll end up buying a trashed car." She stepped up onto the porch. "It's a shame. Nice car." She shook her head. "Okay, I guess I'll see you tomorrow."

"I'll be here. Thanks for doing this, Ally."

"No problem," she said as she walked to the front door.

"Good night."

She turned and looked at him as she opened the front door but didn't answer. Instead she disappeared inside the small house.

Seth followed the winding road from the Triple Bar Ranch with his spirits high, something he hadn't felt in a long time. Part of it was hope that this crazy idea would somehow come to pass. But another big factor was that he would get to spend some time with Ally Kincaid. He liked everything about her: the way she moved, the silky shoulder-length hair that swirled about the fine features of her face. He could get lost in the brilliance of her sparkling green eyes, the sensuous full mouth.

Best of all was her personality, even if she had given him a lot of grief. She knew who she was. She wasn't coy. She didn't try to cover her true nature with any kind of facade. Whether she liked him or not, that persnickety nature made him want to see more.

He caught the direction of where his mind was going and brought it to a stop. Even if she agreed to this crazy plan, it would be a marriage in name only. There would be no getting close to her, no hope of becoming more to her than a man who shared the same house. Unless…

He arrived at the hotel and fell onto the bed. There were some things he needed to do the next morning before he picked her up. Get a key to the house from Kathy, for one. Look at trucks, for another. Ally was right about the car and the gravel roads.

He stood up and pulled off his shirt and pants before heading for the shower. Tomorrow would be a turning point for the research center. His mother had died of leukemia, and he was as determined as he'd ever been about anything to help fund the center. He would still get it built—no doubts there—but the inheritance would speed up the process tenfold. He hoped a miracle happened and Ally said yes.

He knew he was putting a lot of trust in his gut reaction to her, but his gut had never let him down yet. He'd met more than a few self-serving society types who were willing to go so far as fake a pregnancy in order to marry a multimillionaire. He'd been played by the best and so far had kept his bachelor standing intact.

But it was hard to regard Ally as a money-grubber when she'd made it clear she didn't like him at all. Or any of his family. Ironically, that thought was comforting.

# Three

Ally was sitting on the small front porch of her cabin when Seth Masters drove up the next afternoon. It was another beautiful day, and he had the top down on the car. She climbed in, fastened her seat belt and they were off.

She leaned back and looked at the sky, eventually putting her hands above her head, feeling the wind whip through her fingers like a child on her first outing on a merry-go-round. Even though she still didn't trust this man, riding in a car like this on such a perfect day made her feel free.

But as they traveled farther west of Calico Springs, she grew tense. He couldn't possibly be taking her where she thought he was taking her. Could he?

When he turned the car into the long drive between the rows of white fences, she had her answer.

He stopped the car in front of the house and killed the motor. Ally felt his eyes on her, but she sat frozen, staring at her childhood home. Seth exited the car and walked around and opened her door. She accepted his hand as she got out.

"You knew, didn't you?" she said after a long silence.

"I guessed. I saw three ranches yesterday. This was the last one. I liked it a lot and ask who the sellers were. That pretty much gave me the answer." He held up the key. "I thought you might like to see it again."

Ally turned to the house. Her heart was beating out of her chest, and elation battled overwhelming grief in her stomach. She came to a stop at the front steps, not sure if she should go any farther. As though sensing what she was feeling, Seth walked past her and unlocked the door then pushed it open. Stepping inside, she paused and looked around. Everything was as it had been, except several pieces of furniture were gone. Step by step, room by room, she made her way through the house, stopping on occasion to touch an object or the mantel of the fireplace that meant something special to her.

"My mother used to always have a fire in the fireplace here in the kitchen when she cooked on a winter's day. It made the room seem especially warm and cheery."

"It's something not found in many kitchens today."

She turned to face him, her arms wrapped around her chest. "I can tell you unequivocally that this ranch has everything a person would need to be successful in any horse venture. Whether you're looking to breed, train and raise or merely have a few horses to enjoy, you won't go wrong. From the house to the barn to the foaling paddock to the land...it's all here." She swallowed back the tears and tried to talk through her throat that wanted to close. "Are you serious about buying it?"

"I am."

"I guess I'm a little confused. Being part of the Masters family, don't you already own it?"

"In a manner of speaking. It's owned by the family conglomerate, Masters International, LLC. If I decide I want it as my own personal property, I contact my brothers, usually Cole because he handles all property management, and put in a request. He'll pull it from the market and transfer the deed to my name. He's done it for me one other time. Of course, if I do nothing, it can and probably will be sold to someone else outside the family."

She didn't know if that idea made her happy or sad. It would still belong to a Masters, but maybe he was different. It was the best she could hope for. Seeing her home again drew the heartache into a large black mass inside her chest. The pain returned as sure and quick as the day she'd received the notice of foreclosure. But she refused to cry even though the tears filled her eyes. She wouldn't let them fall. It was pointless. She didn't want Seth Masters to think she was using a ruse or poor-little-me syndrome to get her house from him. If it was meant to be hers, she would find a way to get it back without relying on sympathy.

"It really depends on you."

She frowned at the absurd comment. "What? How could you buying this ranch have anything to do with me?"

He hesitated before walking over to lean against the kitchen cabinet then looked at her deeply.

"First of all, you were right in suspecting I was kin to Wade, Cole and Chance. They are my half brothers."

"I knew there was a relation." At least he was admitting it. Finally.

"What you don't know is about a month ago my brothers and I were notified of the probate of our father's will."

"I still don't see what any of that has to do with me."

"I have the plans ready to start building a research facility in California. The money I get from the estate could put me well ahead of the game. The center is badly needed. The research will primarily focus on finding a cure for leukemia." He paused. "My problem is, according to Mr. Rucker, any of the heirs who aren't married by the time the will is probated won't receive an inheritance."

"So…let me get this straight. You need someone to pose as your wife long enough to obtain money." She thought she saw him grimace.

"Put that way, it sounds underhanded and conniving. But most of what I inherit will go to the center. You can see the plans if you have any doubt of that. Or I can put you in touch with my partners, who are doing their part to get this building up and running." He paused, giving that time to soak in. "And it wouldn't be just pretending to be my wife. It must be a legal marriage."

"Surely you know someone who would agree to marry you."

"No. Because of my schedule, there's no time or place for a woman in my life on a permanent basis. I don't know of anyone I would trust to say 'I do' then walk away a few months later, not expecting anything more than what was stipulated in our original agreement."

"But you think you can trust me?" she said, picking up on his idea. "You don't even know me, Masters."

He shrugged. "Call it a gut feeling. When I realized this was your home, I felt it worthy of asking just how badly you want your ranch back. And if you'd be willing to marry me for a few months in order to get it. It would fulfill the terms of my inheritance, and you would have your ranch."

"It's preposterous."

"It's a crazy idea," he agreed. Silence settled over them before he continued. "So, will you marry me, Ally Kincaid?"

That took the breath from her lungs. The man re-

ally was crazy. Like she would ever marry a stranger.
The very idea was ludicrous. Insane.

"Of course," he began, "it would be temporary. I
figure about three months should do it. I'll need to
check with Mr. Rucker on that. But when it's over, I
head back to LA with some money to go toward my
research center, and you have a clear deed to your
ranch in your name. We both win."

"I thought you wanted a ranch or a small farm
for yourself."

He shrugged. "I do. But I can always find another one."

He made it sound so simple. She looked at Seth
Masters for a long time. "How do I know I can trust
you? How do I know if I agree you will give me my
ranch when you get your money? How do I know if
you're a decent, honorable man? You could up and
walk out and leave me with nothing. Hell, I would
be worse off than I am now."

"Mr. Rucker," he stated. "He can attest to who I
am. And I can fly my legal staff in to prepare the
document. Exactly like a prenuptial agreement, in
writing and completely aboveboard. You won't lose
this time, Ally."

"What about you? What if we do this and it ends
up that you don't receive any money from the estate? I mean, do you know for sure you'll get any
funding?"

"It's a gamble. But I'm willing to risk it."

"That research center is really important to you,

huh?" She frowned, only now realizing what Seth was willing to put on the line.

"It's become my life. It's worth taking the risk."

She looked around the familiar room, the walls calling to her. "How soon would you want to do this?"

"As soon as documents can be prepared. Kathy Chisum, the real estate agent, said they have already had quite a lot of interest. If we don't make a decision—correction, if *you* don't make a decision—pretty quick, the ranch might be sold to someone else and we both lose. The probate hearing is on the eleventh, which is eight days from now."

She thought about his offer. Without it, she knew realistically she had little to no chance she would ever come home again. Was thinking his plan might work merely a measure of desperation?

"No," she said finally. "Thanks for the offer, I guess. But no. I'll have to pass."

For the longest time, there was silence in the room.

"Then, if you're ready, I guess we should head back."

Why did she feel as though the breath had been knocked from her lungs? As they made their way to the front door, the walls seemed to call to her. She remembered the last time she'd walked out of this house, fearing she would never see it again, leaving behind cherished childhood memories. Memories of her father. Her mother. Even her first horse. And now she had the chance to come home permanently and she'd turned it down.

It still wasn't too late. She could have it…if she believed in Seth Masters. If she trusted him. Something she had no reason to do. *He is a Masters*, she reminded herself. *You're making the right decision.*

Why, then, did it feel so wrong?

He dropped her at her little house without mentioning it again. There was no attempt to convince her to go along with his plan, no telling her she was making a huge mistake, no pleading with her to change her mind or give it additional thought. He bade her good-night, thanked her for her time and disappeared back down the driveway through the trees.

It occurred to her she didn't know how to find him. But why would she want to find him? She wouldn't let herself dwell on the answer to that question. She'd made the right decision. It was a scheme formulated by a member of the Masters family, and she was correct in turning it down flat. Was this what had happened to her father? Had Reginald Masters offered him something that meant so much to her dad that he'd gambled everything on an outcome that Mr. Masters knew would never happen? If so, in the end it had cost them everything. The ranch was taken, and her father died of a massive heart attack knowing he'd lost it all. She couldn't go through it again. She couldn't. Parting from the ranch a second time was more than she could deal with.

Trust had to be earned. Seth Masters had done

nothing to prove himself. If he was setting her up and if she went for it, it would only confirm she was as big a fool as her father. Masters would laugh all the way back to LA.

She dropped down on her small, well-worn sofa. It was either the cruelest thing she'd ever experienced or the chance of a lifetime. Either way, it was done. She had to let it go. But why would he do such a thing if he wasn't serious? It was a very expensive joke. She couldn't figure out the catch, but there had to be one.

Grabbing her cell, she punched in Ben Rucker's phone number.

"Ben," she said when he came on the phone. "This is Ally Kincaid. What can you tell me about Seth Masters?"

All Ben would say was that Seth was an entrepreneur and sat on the boards of two large regional hospitals in Los Angeles. He couldn't attest to the man's nature, but he'd made a positive impression.

What did that mean? *Positive.* So he was a good liar?

By the end of the next day, Ally was exhausted. On the ranch, she'd made all sorts of stupid, thoughtless mistakes, and when you were working with twelve-hundred-pound horses, stupid mistakes could turn deadly in a heartbeat. But that was what happened when she didn't get any sleep. The night before, she'd lain in bed, tossing and turning, picturing herself in her home, in her own barn. She remembered the silence of the evenings when a cooling summer breeze swept over the land. She remembered the sound of the horses eating their grain with an occasional low nicker, the smells of sweet alfalfa and leather. Those same sounds and smells were here, too, but they were somehow different. It just wasn't the same. It never would be. She remembered the pride she'd known when a client or a buyer came to pick up their new future champion, one that she'd bred and trained.

Once back in her cabin for the night, she forced herself to eat a sandwich. Then, stepping into the shower, she relaxed under the warm spray. She had to let it go. The whole idea of marrying a stranger was unconscionable. What if he was abusive? Or had any number of undesirable qualities?

What if he didn't?

Then she asked herself another question. What if he'd found someone else to marry? He was certainly attractive enough. Most women would probably jump into his arms and hope they stopped by a bedroom on the way to the altar. All he would have to do was show them that grin.

Just as she stepped from the shower, the lights flickered, and a long, low rumble of thunder passed overhead. Usually she loved the rain. Not tonight. It made her aware of how lonely she was. She looked at her bed then glanced around to her closet. Was it go to bed for another sleepless night or grab a fresh pair of jeans and a shirt and see if she could track down Seth Masters? There were only three hotels in Calico Springs…

An hour later the rain pelted her as she entered the front lobby of the Calico Springs Hotel and Suites. Soon she was standing in front of room 214. Without allowing herself a chance to back out, she raised her hand and knocked.

A couple of minutes later, Seth Masters pulled open the door. Bare to his waist, dressed only in formfitting jeans, he leaned one muscled arm against the door frame and looked surprised to see her.

"Ms. Kincaid?" He opened the door wider.

"Yes." Ally swallowed hard. "And yes. I will marry you, Mr. Masters," she said, "as long as that document conveys what you told me."

"It will."

"So what do we do now?"

He backed up to let her in, that sexy grin on his face. "First, let's get you dry."

"And then?"

"And then…tomorrow I'll have my attorney fly in, and while you provide the information for the legal agreement, I'll arrange to buy the property."

"Just like that. You're going to buy the ranch."

"Just like that."

Ally had never believed in fairy tales, but if this proposition was real and not some cruel joke, she was living in one.

Seth's attorney, James Buchanan, and his legal assistant arrived by two o'clock the following day, ready to get to work. The fact that Seth let Ally set the conditions gave her added confidence in what she had agreed to do. Ally had no problem with clauses that precluded her from any claim on Seth's current holdings. Fair was fair. The only thing she wanted was her ranch.

At some point during the afternoon, it finally hit her: she was getting married. Married to a man she didn't know. At twenty-four years old, she'd honestly never thought about getting married. While her friends in school planned and daydreamed about that special day, Ally's thoughts had been of horses and taking the winning trophy at quarter horse competitions. All that changed in seconds when she agreed to say "I do."

The following day Seth picked her up and drove to the county clerk's office, where they applied for the wedding license. In two days' time, she'd become Ally Masters.

It was an unbelievable situation, one that would have her father rolling over in his grave if he knew. She put it out of her mind and kept telling herself that Seth wasn't a real Masters. He was from Los Angeles and not in cahoots with the local members of the family. Sometimes it worked for a few minutes. Then at other times she would look at Seth and see shades of his father and the truth came screaming back at her of how closely Seth was related to the Masters patriarch who had betrayed them, the man who'd taken them for all they had and left her alone struggling to survive.

What was she doing?

* * *

Two days later the civil ceremony was a short, no-frills affair. Mr. Buchanan and his legal assistant served as the witnesses. The surprise came when Seth extracted a black velvet box from his pocket that contained a beautiful diamond-encrusted wedding ring and slipped it onto Ally's finger. Then he handed her a solid gold band to be placed on his hand, and with a few words from the county judge, they were pronounced husband and wife.

When Seth took her into his arms, their eyes met and the world tipped a little. Ever so slowly Seth lowered his lips to hers. His kiss was gentle, almost soothing. Reassuring. Ally became lost in his touch, in his strong arms. The kiss felt like something more meaningful than a token kiss at a fake wedding ceremony.

Seth lost no time in taking it to the next level, his mouth closing over hers, his tongue entering and tasting, letting her taste him. When they finally drew apart, she glanced up at his face as he released her and caught a twinkle in his amber eyes. Her heart thumped a few hard beats. She hoped she saw merriment in his eyes, that the twinkle didn't represent the dreaded *gotcha*.

Either way, it was done. Because land acquisitions and sales were handled by a special department in Masters International, LLC., it was not necessary for any of the Masters brothers to be present for the transfer of the deed. Seth had received a phone call that morning from Cole, welcoming him to the neighborhood. There were three days until the purchase of the ranch was finalized. Another few days until the probate hearing. A few months until he would return to his life in LA. *You can handle a few months.* What would happen between now and then was anyone's guess. The only thing she was assured of was that the ranch would be hers. Nothing else mattered.

Returning the waves from Mr. Buchanan and his legal assistant, she let Seth escort her out to his car.

"Are you hungry?" he asked. "It's almost five o'clock. Care to grab a bite to eat?"

"Sure. Whatever you'd like to do."

She saw him purse his lips to subdue a grin.

Soon they were seated across from each other at a small table in Burdall's café. Ally couldn't help but remember the last time they were here. Then, she didn't even know his name. Now, his last name was hers. *Masters.* She eyed the glittering diamonds on her left hand.

"You went to a lot of unnecessary expense," she commented. "The ring is beautiful."

Seth shrugged. "I guess I'm a bit old-fashioned. I couldn't see not giving my bride a ring for the ceremony."

*My bride.*

"Well, I'll certainly return it to you before you leave."

"I'm not worried about it." He sat back while the waitress placed glasses of ice water on the table and took their order. "So…where are we going to spend the night?"

"Excuse me?"

"Your place or mine?"

"Ah… I thought we would each go back to our own previous living arrangements. You at your hotel and me at the cabin."

"Not really indicative of a newlywed couple. Remember, this has got to look as real as it is on paper. For all intents and purpose, as far as anyone knows we are in love. Any doubts someone might raise as to the legality of our union might challenge my rights to be considered in the will. In which case, all bets are off."

Ally could feel the irritation like a slow burn inside. Regardless of what she'd agreed to on paper, she'd never given thought to having to spend the night…nights…with this man. "You never said anything about sleeping together."

He looked at her, dumbfounded. "I didn't think it necessary. We are, in fact, legally married. Why bother to tie the knot if you live on one side of town and I stay on the other?"

"Did you or did you not tell me we had to put up a good front when we're out in public? That does not hold true behind closed doors."

"Why?"

She leaned over the table toward him. "You know why," she shot back.

"Do most married couples not stay together? Share living arrangements?"

The waitress set their plates down on the table. The steak appeared cooked to perfection, but she knew if she tried to eat at this moment, she would choke. Her throat was closing until she could barely breathe.

"Yes," she hissed. "But we are not most couples!"

"Ally, you're getting upset over nothing. Just because we share a home doesn't mean something will necessarily happen between us. Don't get me wrong—" he began to cut his steak "—I'm on board if it does. You're a very beautiful woman. But it's your call."

"Share a home? You mean you intend to move into the house on the ranch?"

Seth looked at her as though she'd told a really bad joke.

"Fine. We can go to my cabin. It has a twin-size bed and a sofa." He had to be at least six foot two, with broad shoulders. There was little doubt that if he tried to sleep on either the bed or couch, his head would hang off one end and his feet the other. "You can take your pick."

"When do you have to be out of the cabin?"

"I have it as long as I keep my job, which I intend to do."

"That doesn't make any sense."

"What do you expect me to do? Live in a tree?"

"I expect you to give your resignation and move to your ranch. Isn't that what you wanted?"

"I can't move to the ranch until you close on the property."

"Which is the day after tomorrow."

"Regardless, in the meantime I need someplace to live. Plus, I need my salary. Jobs in this area are not plentiful."

"You don't need a job. I can supply anything you need. Which reminds me, we are going to need some furniture for the house. In the meantime, we'll stay at the hotel. Or, if you prefer, we can go on a short honeymoon."

"That's ludicrous."

"It's expected."

"Not by me!"

The simmer was back. He expected her to act like the blushing bride and go off to some strange place with him? Not happening.

"Look, Masters." She quickly looked around them to ensure they weren't being overheard then lowered her voice. "I'll play this game only so far. I have zero intentions of getting into bed with a man I've known less than a week. You flatter yourself if you think I can be coerced into such a thing. If that's what you believe, you picked the wrong woman."

"Mrs. Masters, I never said anything about sharing a bed. That was your own idea. One I'm not opposed to but not one I suggested. We will, however, share accommodations. If you want to explain to your friends and cohorts why we spent our wedding night in a cabin that's barely large enough for one person, so be it."

"I had no intention of telling anyone about this sham marriage. That's your thing, not mine."

"I don't care if you spread the news or not, but this is a small town. Sooner or later someone will recognize you and ask about the man you're with. What are you going to say then?"

Why hadn't she considered all of this before she signed that stupid contract? Suddenly the ranch didn't seem all that important. A fleeting picture flashed in her mind of her lying on a feather-soft bed with Seth's strong arms around her. Of snuggling there, warm and protected. A flare of heat bloomed in her lower region, and she crossed her legs to fight off the sensation. It didn't help.

"Fine. Have it your way. We can go to your hotel and I'll take the couch or the floor."

He smiled and put a bite of steak in his mouth. "It's not a very big couch."

"I don't care." She sprinkled some salt over her baked potato and began to eat.

"You might after a few nights."

"I'll be fine. Don't worry about me. Just keep to your side of the room and do not come into mine."

At that he smiled then pursed his lips as though to keep from grinning outright.

"Whatever you say, Mrs. Masters."

# Four

Seth recalled a time from his childhood when he'd been scratched by a neighbor's cat. He had a strange feeling he'd just taken on one again, only this time the feline was taller and its claws twice as sharp. Still, he loved a challenge. He had no intention of making any moves on her, but she kept bringing up the subject. Maybe he should give making love to the fiery redhead a bit more thought. She was a beautiful woman, and the idea was tantalizing.

"Do you want to go and look at some furniture tomorrow?" Seth asked, changing the subject. "How about we check out some furniture stores in the afternoon?"

"Okay," she replied. "The mattresses at the house are old. We're gonna need places to sleep."

"And a refrigerator. Stove. Kitchen table. You might want to look for a sofa or a couple of easy chairs to go in the den as well."

She laid her fork down and met his gaze. "Why are you doing this?"

"Because I don't happen to like sleeping on the floor. However, if you do I'll simply purchase a couple of air mattresses and call it done."

"No," she said after a time. "A bed would be nice. As would a stove and refrigerator. I just don't know how long it will be until I can pay you back."

"I don't recall saying you had to pay me back. Anyway, don't sweat the small stuff. We'll figure it out."

After dinner Ally agreed to show him around the area. It was prime land, with beef cows and horses dotting the horizon. Pine and oak trees towered at the edges of the vast pastureland. A river wound its way through the hills and close to the small town at the center of it all.

"Were you born here?"

"Yeah. I spent a few years in College Station northeast of Austin while I was in school, but that's about it. What about you? Born and raised in Los Angeles?"

He nodded. "But I've always craved the country. A place you can see forever and take a deep breath."

"Why didn't you leave or move farther out of the city?"

"I would have liked to. California has some of the most beautiful places to live in the United States.

But there wasn't time to think about it. Generally I'm on call 24-7. Many times I have to fly out on a minute's notice."

"That's gotta be rough. You must really like what you do."

Seth nodded. "I especially like the fact that it gives me the opportunity to work on projects like the research center. A friend of mine is a hematologist. Another is an oncologist. We are combining efforts toward our goals. They are so close to developing a cure for a lot of diseases. I want to help push that research forward." He was quiet for a moment, unsure of how much to tell her about his past. "My mother died of leukemia. I promised her I would help find a cure."

He caught Ally's gaze; her eyes shimmered with understanding. "I'm sorry."

"It was a few years back. But thank you."

When they turned back toward the ranch where she worked, it was already growing dark. Seth helped her out of the car in front of the small cabin that was nestled in the trees within the borders of the ranch.

"I just have to grab a few things," she told him as she got out of the car. "I won't be long."

Seth watched her disappear inside then followed. As he looked around, he was a bit surprised at what he saw. The single room was even smaller than it looked from the outside. There was a sink, a commode and a tiny shower stall in one corner, and a closet without any doors in the other. In the center of the room was a single bed, along with a tiny moth-eaten sofa and one straight chair against the wall. Having seen the house where she'd grown up, it was a shock to him that she now had to make do with such poor accommodations.

She looked up from packing and saw him standing inside the door. "I don't have a suitcase. Pillowcases will have to do. Tomorrow if I need anything else, I can probably find a box."

Seth nodded and kept his thoughts to himself. She would not be coming back to this place no matter what he had to do to prevent it. She needed clothes and a good bed and enough space to turn around. From her strong attitude, he would never have guessed she was living in such deplorable conditions. He walked over and picked up the first pillowcase she'd filled.

"I'll take this to the car. Take your time."

When they arrived at the hotel, Seth helped her carry two filled pillowcases inside. The suite wasn't a big room by his standards but three times the size of her cabin. But there was only one bed. A quick phone call to the hotel office confirmed what he feared: they were fully booked. It was Friday night. No two-bed rooms available.

"There are hangers in the closet, extra pillows in that cabinet." He pointed to a closet door. "And extra blankets, I think." He couldn't keep from glancing over to the small, curved sofa. He should be a gentleman and offer to sleep there, but at the same time, he saw no reason they couldn't share the California king. If she insisted on using the little sofa, that was her decision.

Ally stood in the center of the room looking lost, as though she didn't know what to do next. He found her timidity charming. According to her driver's license, which he'd seen when they applied for the marriage certificate, she was twenty-four. Most of the women he knew wouldn't think twice about stripping down and crawling into the bed. It made him curious what her previous life had been like. Married and divorced? Engaged? Maybe a few boyfriends here and there but nothing serious? As beautiful as she was, he found that hard to believe.

A glance at his watch told him it was almost midnight. It had been a long day. He suspected it had been a long and emotional one for Ally. Walking into the bedroom, he pulled back the covers with one hand while he loosened his tie with the other.

"You're welcome to first shot at the bathroom. There are extra towels and bathrobes in the small pantry in the dressing room."

"Thanks," she said and turned in that direction, disappearing behind the closed door. The bath had a large whirlpool bathtub. He hoped she would partake and let some of the tension ease out of her body. He couldn't help but smile when he heard her turn on the tap.

Sometime later she emerged wearing an old T-shirt that hung a few inches above her knees. Her hair had been washed and dried and fell in feather-soft layers around her head. He grew hard despite the control he tried for. Her full lips were closed tight; not even a hint of a smile touched her features. She pulled a blanket and pillow from the closet and set about making up the tiny sofa. By the time Seth was finished in the bathroom, she was perched on the makeshift bed in the main room, looking as though she was in deep thought.

Curled under her blanket, she looked miserable.

"Are you sure you don't want to share the bed?"

"I'm fine."

With a sigh Seth turned off the light next to the bed. Short of picking her up and physically putting her on the bed, there wasn't a lot more he could do. He had a feeling the little feline would show her claws big-time if he tried it. He loosened the string on his sweatpants and closed the adjoining door.

The next morning Seth woke up to an empty room. Then he found the note on the nightstand next to where he slept. *Gone to work. Back at six.* He grabbed his cell and looked at the time. It was barely seven in the morning. Ally worked twelve-hour days?

He showered, got dressed and headed to the ranch where Ally worked, stopping along the way for a to-go breakfast and coffee. When he arrived at the Triple Bar Ranch, he found her at the back of the main barn lunging a chestnut yearling in one of the exercise pens. He stepped over and held out a sausage biscuit and a cup of coffee.

She walked over to where he stood against the corral fence and took the coffee and biscuit. "Thanks."

"No problem. Are you going to talk to your boss today about leaving?"

"No," she told him hesitantly. "I'll quit only after you can tell me the house is yours. Or mine." She shook her head. "You know what I mean."

"You can trust me, Ally."

"Time will tell."

"How about this afternoon we head to Calico Springs and see if we can decide on some furniture?"

"I have to work."

"I close on the property tomorrow. What are you going to sleep on if we don't get some beds?"

"I was reconsidering, thinking I'll just stay here."

Seth sighed. "Why purchase the farm if you don't want to be there? Was I mistaken to think you wanted your ranch?"

"No. But—"

"No buts. If you don't want your ranch, tell me now."

He knew what she was thinking: she wanted her ranch, but without him.

"I'll be ready at noon. Thanks for breakfast."

Seth nodded. "I'll call my assistant in LA and have her arrange for some housekeepers. Setting up that house is going to be a big undertaking."

"How much help is needed to tell the delivery people where to put two beds and a stove and re-frigerator?"

"I had in mind a little more than that."

The filly began to paw, anxious to return to the barn or pasture. Ally broke off a small piece of the biscuit and fed it to the young horse, which seemed to soothe its impatience somewhat. Dropping the remains of the biscuit into the sack, she took another sip of the coffee and handed the cup and bag back to Seth.

"How did you know I liked cream in my coffee?"

"Just a guess," he answered as he took the empty sack. "I'll pick you up about noon."

Ally watched him walk away from the corral, his long strides carrying him down the graveled road to his car.

He was a strange man. She didn't as yet have him figured out. His looks were what she'd always pictured someone from California would look like: tanned and muscled with blond highlights in his hair where the sun hit it. His face was strikingly handsome, with laugh lines around the edges of his mouth and dimples when he smiled. His wealth should have made him arrogant, but she still hadn't seen any sign of that. He almost blended in with the locals, people she'd known most of her life. Strange. The other Masters brothers had grown up in Calico Springs. Someone who didn't know him would assume Seth had as well.

He came back at noon, and they went shopping. The first stop was to a car dealership, where Seth picked out a new pickup truck. Then they went to shop for furniture and some household necessities.

"Don't you want to try out the mattress before you

make your decision?" Seth asked Ally, standing next to a row of floor models.

"I'm sure whatever you select will be fine."

"At least sit on it. Ultimately you will be the one who keeps and sleeps on the mattress when you take over the house. You might as well pick out what you like."

*Humor him*, she thought, *and move on.* She sat down on the closest display model and immediately didn't like it. She moved to a second then a third. By the time she found one she liked, they were at the opposite end of the large showroom.

"That's it?" Seth asked. "That's the one?"

"Yeah."

"Send out two, both king," he said to the sales associate. "Now let's find bedroom suites to go with them."

"How do you know you'll like the mattress I picked out?"

He looked around the huge showroom, which was on the third floor of the shop, and at all the mattresses she'd tried out. "I doubt I could do better. Come on."

Together they went to the second floor, where they purchased two bedroom suites, a living room suite, a kitchen table and chairs, and loungers for the den.

"I'll have the list of items we bought sent to Karen, my assistant, and tell her to fill in the rest. Anything she misses we can get later," Seth said as he gave Ally a ride back to work.

When they got back to Triple Bar Ranch, he told

her he'd pick her up at seven, take her back to the hotel to change and they'd go out to dinner.

Head spinning, all Ally could think was, *What have I gotten myself into?*

"So tomorrow you're a ranch owner," Ally said as the waitress set her dinner plate in front of her. She put her napkin in her lap and picked up the fork.

"Tomorrow the deed will be transferred to my name. I don't have to be there. It's all handled internally within the company." He took a sip of his coffee.

A rush of goose bumps covered her skin. What must it be like to be able to obtain a ranch with no more concern for the cost than she would have buying a can of beans at the grocery store? Granted, Seth didn't write a check for the purchase price but he could have had it been necessary. She hadn't been raised in poverty—far from it. But this was new to her.

"A can of beans."

"Excuse me?" Seth asked.

"You buy a five-hundred-acre ranch as easily as I would buy a can of beans."

He grinned. "Firstly, I didn't actually buy it. No money changed hands. The company has over one hundred thousand acres in Texas alone so this wasn't a big deal. And secondly, isn't that what families do for each other?"

She opened her mouth but no words would come

out. Then, "Okay. Sure. You've got me there. The next time I need a cup of sugar I'll know who to call."

Seth's baritone laughter rang out over the restaurant.

Seth had chosen a new restaurant located along the banks of the Calico River. They'd been given a table next to the wall of glass overlooking the water, which shimmered with a silver glow from the lights along the banks. A small candle in a glass chimney spread its ambient light across their table. Looking up at Seth, she was once again drawn in by the handsome planes of his face. The deep laugh lines on either side of his mouth added to the overall integrity of his features. His dark brows seem to bring out the golden flecks in his brown eyes. As her gaze dropped to his generous lips, she realized they were pursed in an effort to hold back a smile.

She immediately focused on her plate and the perfectly prepared steak.

"By this weekend you should be able to start getting the barn ready for the transfer of your horses. I'm sure they'll be glad to be home again. How long has it been?"

"Just over a year."

"You're gonna need someone to help you out, at least at first. Unless you know someone, why don't you stop by the employment office tomorrow and arrange for some cowboys to come to work?"

"I can do anything that needs to be done."

"You can't do it all—check the fences on that much land, repair the barns, do whatever it is you have to do to the stalls, clean out the feed bins, fill up the water tanks—and that's just the parts I know about—besides horses to train. There's probably a lot more to it than I've mentioned. If you need more than three ranch hands, get them."

Ally sat back in her chair and placed her fork by the side of her plate. "Why are you doing this? The agreement was you buy the farm in exchange for me marrying you for three months. There was no furniture involved. Certainly no ranch hands. Right now I barely have the money to buy feed for the horses."

"Then get whatever you need."

"That isn't what I meant. You didn't answer my question," she said, exasperated. "Do you not understand that I don't have the money to repay you for all of this? Marrying you for ninety days hardly gives me carte blanche to your bank account. And right now I have no clue how I'm going to pay you back for what you've already provided."

Seth put his silverware down and folded his hands in front of him, his elbows on the table. "What you're doing for me means a lot, Ally. I don't expect either of us to stay in a practically empty house for three months. The rest is just common sense. I wish you would see it that way. You're paying me by allowing me to be a part of the probate. And before you say it, if my part of the estate turns out to be nothing, you're giving me a chance to try. My mother died from leukemia. I promised her I would find a way to fight it. The research center depends a great deal on the money from the will. Without you there would be no money and no chance for obtaining any."

Ally knew there were a dozen women she could name right off the bat who would jump at the chance to marry Seth Masters. Ironic he would choose the one least interested. She consciously relaxed. She had a document, signed and notarized, that would ensure his agreement was honored. He had the same. All she had to do was get through three months. As to the household furnishings, she'd explained she couldn't afford what he seemed intent on buying. She had no choice but to let him buy what he wanted and hope they could settle in the end.

He was a man's man. A rugged, self-assured, no-nonsense kind of guy who looked every bit of his million dollars. Maybe billion dollars.

"Okay. I'll say no more about it."

"Good. How is your steak?"

"It's good."

By the time they arrived back at the hotel, she was exhausted, more from emotional stress than physical exertion. Dropping her purse on the small sofa, she grabbed a clean T-shirt and headed straight for the shower. They had accomplished a lot. Tomorrow Seth would close on the ranch. Then, in a few days, he'd deal with the probate of the will. Understanding his need for additional funding for the research center made her look at him in a different light. For the first time she began to see him as someone who cared, not just a millionaire who wanted more. His mother's death must have been devastating. She could relate after losing her dad and having no one. No siblings, no family. He had his brothers, but how close had they been at the time of her death? She hoped the probate went well for him.

After a quick shower, she dressed in the oversize T-shirt and returned to the main living area. Making her small bed on the sofa took no time. She lay down and wiggled, trying to find a comfortable spot, plumped her pillow and closed her eyes. Sleep when it came was not restful. She tossed and turned. And it was cold. She tugged the blanket around her, but it did little to help in the cool room. A thought drifted across her mind that she should get up and adjust the thermostat, but instead she lapsed into a troubled sleep.

The warmth that surrounded her was heavenly. A heavy weight rested over her waist, while delicious heat met her back and legs. The feel of silken sheets beneath her stirred her to consciousness. A hard mound pressed against her lower back. Slowly she opened her eyes and immediately knew where she was. On the bed. In Seth's arms. His erection pressed against her. How she got there wasn't clear. She heard his deep, even breathing and tried to slow her speeding heart. Hoping not to disturb him, she lifted the covers from over her and slowly moved his arm from around her waist. Before she could slip to the edge of the bed, his arm was back wrapped around her as his large body nestled her closely, his hot breath against her neck. Good grief. He must think she was a pillow. This was not good. She didn't want to be in his arms when he woke up. She didn't want to be in his arms, period. While her mind raced to figure out what to do, she heard his breathing change.

"Good morning." His deep voice caused goose pimples to flash down her spine.

Ally immediately sat up, threw the covers back and slipped out from under his arms. The room had a slight chill, and for an instant she wanted to go back to the warm nest they'd formed during the night. Instead she walked into the main room where her jeans lay on the sofa, grabbing them and her shirt.

"Good morning," she replied, looking at him suspiciously. He was still lying on his side in the bed, his arm propped on top on the pillow, his head resting on his hand. His hair was tousled. The five o'clock shadow gave him a devilish look that was highlighted by his eyes. His full lips were open, showing strong white teeth. It looked as though he'd found a tasty morsel in his lair and wanted to devour her piece by piece. She watched as his eyes roamed over her.

She swallowed hard as her body blossomed with heat that sizzled from her lips all the way down to her core. This was not a man who would be happy to be her new best friend. He knew a woman's body, and he wouldn't hesitate to show her just how well he knew her if she gave him the least bit of enticement. Which she did not intend to do.

"Do I need to ask how I came to be in your bed?" She seriously doubted she had made her way there in her sleep, and she darned sure didn't do it on purpose.

"I found you on the floor. You'd lost your blanket. You were cold. Rather than go through the hassle of getting you stuffed back onto that tiny couch, it just seemed logical to pick you up and put you in bed. I made sure you were warm and went back to sleep."

"Well. Thank you for that. I think. Excuse me," she said as she turned and marched to the bathroom, still clutching her clean clothes.

How was she going to make it through three months of this?

Two days later excitement overtook her common sense when it came to her job. Why train horses for someone else when all she wanted to do was be in her childhood home and get her own ranch up and running again? After Seth gave her his assurances, she tendered her resignation at the Triple Bar Ranch. Then they were on their way to the farm. Her farm. Seth's farm. She wouldn't be honest with herself if she didn't admit to having misgivings that she'd come to rely on Seth a little too much. She was putting her future in the hands of a man she really didn't know, trusting him when he told her everything would be okay. Trusting him when his father had brought all of her hardship to bear. Knowing her heart was becoming involved scared her the most.

The cleaning ladies arrived around ten o'clock, and after receiving instructions from Ally, they set to work.

By two o'clock, the furniture arrived. And at the end of the day, Ally put aside her own cleaning implements, feeling a sense of accomplishment for the first time in a very long time.

"It all looks good," Seth said as he entered the kitchen where she was unpacking a box of dishes his personal assistant had bought online and arranged to have shipped. They'd also received linens, cookware and three other large boxes of miscellaneous items.

"It's getting there," Ally agreed. "The new furniture will fit in the house perfectly. I still need to finish unpacking and buy some groceries."

"You can do that tomorrow while I'm at Ben's office."

"Oh! I'd forgotten. Tomorrow is the reading of the will. I hope it goes well for you. Do you know your half brothers very well?"

He nodded. "Well enough, I suppose. I've been coming here every summer since I was six. Spent a couple of Christmas holidays with them. That pretty much stopped when I went to college, but we've kept in touch."

"I've never had any direct dealings with them," Ally said. "When I lost my ranch, it was handled by corporate attorneys and your father. I never met any of your brothers. I hope they are not as bloodthirsty as your father. I'm sorry, but that's what he was to me."

"I understand. I had a different impression of him, though under different circumstances, I could see how he'd be somewhat cold." Seth said. "But I've never found my brothers to be anything like that."

"Good. Seth? Try not to worry about tomorrow. I

know how important it is for you, but believe it will go as planned. No reason why it shouldn't, right?"

"You never know. I hope you're right." He looked at her as if he'd seen a whole new side of her. But maybe she was just being ridiculous. "Thanks for the encouragement."

"Of course," she responded. For a long moment their gazes caught, and neither moved to break the eye contact. "Well, I need to go to the barn and check on the progress out there."

Ally strove to make her heartbeat slow down. Seth was just standing there, his thumbs hanging from his jeans pockets, the long-sleeved shirt rolled to just below his elbows, and those eyes so brown, the flakes of gold glinting. He had her pulse hammering. He was so male. Extra stamina was needed to avoid falling for this guy. Still, she couldn't help but ask, "Want to come with me?"

"Sure."

Together they walked toward the large, sprawling barn, and for the second time in as many days, Ally wondered what she'd gotten herself into.

# Five

The town square was brimming with activity when Seth arrived for the meeting at Ben Rucker's office the next day. He had just found a parking spot when he heard his name being called in a deep voice like his own.

"Seth!" He turned to see Wade and Cole walking down the sidewalk toward him.

"How in the hell are you doing?" Cole said as he gave Seth a quick hug and solid pat on the back. Wade held his hand out to him and shook it warmly, followed by a friendly pat on his shoulder.

"It's been a long time," said Wade, smiling broadly.

"It has," Seth answered. "It's good to see you both again. Where's Chance?"

"He's on his way. Had a mare unexpectedly go

into labor and said he needed to make sure all was okay. He called a few minutes ago and said he was en route."

"Good. It will be good to see him."

"So, how have you been? I was sorry to hear about your mother."

"Thanks. Yeah, she fought a brave battle, but…"

"So now you're building a cancer research center?"

"That's the plan." He should have been surprised that Wade and Cole knew about his project, but Wade tended to keep abreast of everything that touched the family.

"I hope it goes well for you today," Wade told him just as a white pickup truck slid up next to the curb. A tall, lanky man got out, a smile of welcome clearly etched on his face.

"I know you… I think we've met before," Chance teased as he reached Seth.

"Could be," Seth returned. "How have you been?" He extended his hand.

"Couldn't ask for better, brother. And you?"

"Doing good."

"We should all get together with the wives before you leave," Cole suggested. "How long are you here?"

"I'd planned on it just being a couple of weeks, but that's changing. I got a ranch. A small repo you guys were sitting on. Went through the LLC. Cole said it was fine. We're setting up house. I wanted a place closer to my family."

"Well all right," Chance said, giving his approval. "It's about time."

"I appreciate that. My wife had her heart set on this place west of town," Seth said. "At least being in the county will afford me the opportunity to see more of you guys when we all happen to be in town."

"And speaking of wives, when are we all going to get to meet her? And I don't think you've met my Laurel. We need to get together while we are all here," Wade said, and everyone agreed.

They talked for a few more minutes until it was time to go inside Ben Rucker's office. When they were all seated in the small conference room, Mr. Rucker began to go over the terms of the will. Seth was made a full partner in Masters International Inc., plus awarded a substantial cash endowment. He fought to keep the tears of happiness from clouding his eyes. It was better than he'd hoped.

Their father had divided the bulk of the estate among the four brothers, less bequests to charities and personal contributions to a smattering of individuals Seth didn't know. In short, he was now a billionaire. Their business would envelop his own companies, and he would work through the conglomerate company on his own endeavors plus take on some of the responsibilities of Masters International Inc. The main thing was the research clinic would now be fully funded, something he felt overwhelmingly grateful for.

"Seth," Wade said as they exited Ben Rucker's office. "We were thinking about getting together Saturday night. It's rare we're all here at the same time. We would love to meet your wife. And I don't think you've met my wife, Laurel. Are you free?"

"I would like to say yes, but let me check with Ally. Can I give you a call?"

"Absolutely. Hopefully we will see you both then."

"It's nothing fancy," Chance added. "Just some burgers and steaks out on the veranda. Jeans and T-shirts will be fine."

They all shook hands and got into their separate cars. Seth drove to his new ranch, hoping Ally was there.

When he got back to the ranch, he met a delivery truck leaving just before he reached the driveway. He parked and headed for the door. Letting himself in, he immediately noticed that the painters had done an excellent job. The draperies had been freshened. The old furniture they'd chosen to keep had been cleaned, and some of the new furniture was already in place.

"Anybody home? Ally?" he called from just inside the foyer.

"She's out at the barn." A middle-aged woman with a kind smile came out from the kitchen down the hall and greeted him. "I'm Pauline Haddock, your new housekeeper. I live in Calico Springs." She offered her hand, which Seth accepted. "That wife of yours loves her horses."

Seth grinned. "Yes, she does. Nice to meet you, Pauline." And he turned toward the back door, eager to find his bride.

* * *

"Where do you want these old planks?" Stony Osterman asked. He was one of four ranch hands Seth had hired to help get the barn and land ready for livestock.

"Ya know what?" Ally mused. "Let's make a debris pile outside the barn area where it will be safe to have a fire. We'll just burn the lot as well as the tree trimmings."

"That sounds like a good plan," Stony agreed. He immediately tossed his load of old, worn pine lumber on a spot that didn't have grass and was far away from any buildings and trees.

"Might as well add the old shavings to the pile," Ally said before he could turn away.

"Yes, ma'am," he said before heading to the barn. She could hear his voice as he conveyed the orders to the other three. In just a few minutes, she heard Seth's new tractor start up as it scraped up the pine shavings from the main hall of the barn, carrying them out to the burn site.

"Is this trash day?" Seth asked, smiling as he walked up behind her.

"Yep." Ally couldn't help but smile back. "Thanks to the ranch hands and your tractor, we should have the barn ready for the horses by the end of the week. I never realized so much decay could happen in just over a year."

"Looks like you're going to need some more lumber. Get whatever you need. I'll have my assistant set up an account with the local lumberyard. Are the hands working out?"

Ally nodded. "They're great. All hard workers. No grumblers. We did good."

There was an unmistakable twinkle in Seth's eyes.

"I thought we could just stack the old shavings and lumber out here and have a fire. There's currently no burn ban. If we keep it small, it should burn nicely."

Seth nodded.

"How did the probate go? Do you get to build your research center?"

She was anxious on Seth's behalf. He had already spent so much money on the house and land, and gone to so much trouble to marry her, all in the hope of being part of his father's will.

Seth drew a deep breath. "Good, as I'd hoped. I spoke with Ben Rucker just before the others arrived. He was pleased I'd found a wife. Surprised but tickled to learn it was you."

"Good. Congratulations." Ally smiled.

"This means we can commence building the research center in a couple months. Probably midsummer."

"So…you're a billionaire now?"

"Yeah." He frowned and looked at her questioningly. "Primarily it's tied up in the family corporation, where I'm now a partner, but yeah. I suppose you could say that. Why?"

"I've never known one before. Are you going to get snooty?"

Seth grinned and fought to keep from laughing. "I'll do my best not to. But tell you what. If you see me start to get snooty, I expect you to put me in my place, okay?"

She watched him intently as though not knowing if he was teasing. Then she said, "You can count on it. So, you'll be leaving to oversee construction at your research center."

"Maybe in a week or so," he answered, watching her face. "Most of the plans have been drawn up, and the rest can be handled with Matthew Rundles and John Sizemore, my partners in the center, during a conference call. We have a general contractor, so unless an issue comes up, which I'm always expecting, he will handle everything. I may have to make a couple of trips back to LA over the next few weeks, but that's about it." He tipped his head. "Are you okay with that?"

Ally shrugged. "Sure. No problem here. I mean, it's your business. It's your ranch."

He held her gaze as though he was expecting a different answer but then changed the subject. "Speaking of the ranch, I'm going to need a horse. Could I get your help in finding a good one?"

"Of course, although you're welcome to ride one of mine. They're all very well trained, and I trust you to be gentle with them."

"I'm always gentle. At least when I need to be."

"Yeah, well. With these girls, you have to be. They are very responsive to the lightest touch."

"Like master, like student?"

Ally chanced a look at Seth, and the sparkle in his eyes caused a blush to run up her neck and over her face. She turned away. "I want to show you the house. Are you busy?"

"After you."


Between what was left of the old furniture and the new items they had purchased, the house felt warm and welcoming. He especially liked the den. The sofa and two recliners fit perfectly around the fireplace. It would be a good place to spend a wintry evening.

"Your bed is set up in the master bedroom. Mine is down the hall." She walked toward the stairs, intent on showing him the second floor.

"Why didn't you just have your bed put in the master bedroom?" Seth asked, following behind her. "It will eventually be your house."

Ally shrugged. "It just didn't seem to be the right thing to do."

"Of course, we could always share the same bedroom. That would solve the problem."

"There isn't a problem," she returned and continued up the stairs.

When he caught up, she was in the midst of making the bed in one of the bedrooms. She walked to the edge and grabbed the comforter.

"We have staff to do that. You don't have to make the bed."

She shrugged. "The hands are handling the barn stuff. I didn't have anything else to do."

"Of course not. Just oversee a housekeeper and a barn full of cowboys."

She shrugged. "I wanted to get this bed ready. Mine is down the hall, and Pauline is working in there. The kitchen, den and living room are set up. The stove, new dishwasher and refrigerator are being installed as we speak, and I have a carpenter downstairs making room for a microwave. Hope that was okay. We're going to need a few more pots and pans, but otherwise, it's all set."

"Karen took care of that. Another delivery should arrive tomorrow."

Ally sighed and gave him a rare smile.

"It all looks good. You've done a great job," he said.

She pushed a pillow into a fresh new pillowcase. "Still a lot to do."

He shook his head and smiled. Leave it to him to marry a perfectionist.

"By the way, are you free Saturday evening?"

Ally frowned and shrugged. "I don't know. Why?"

"My brothers want to get together with the wives over dinner—"

"No. No, I can't," she interrupted and hastily made for the door. "Pauline? Could you finish making this bed?"

"Sure thing, Mrs. Masters."

Turning at the upper landing, Ally quickly made her way down the stairs.

"Ally, wait." He hurried after her.

"Gotta go to the barn," she said over her shoulder as she hurried through the kitchen and toward the back door.

"Ally—"

She seemed to quicken her pace and was out the door and halfway across the yard before he could catch her.

"Ally, what's wrong?"

"Nothing. Look, I really have things I need to see to in the barn. The hired hands will need—"

"Whatever they need can wait. I want to know what the sudden flight down the stairs is all about. Is this something to do with the dinner Saturday night?"

Ally stood in front of him, lips drawn into a thin line.

"Do you still hold it against them for what our father did regarding your ranch? Is that it?"

She looked down at her boots. "No. How can I when you've given it back?" She bit her lower lip, a gesture that made him crazy. He wanted to be the one to suckle on those full lips.

"Then what is it?"

She shrugged, peering up at his face, then away. "Look, I'm just a common person. I don't exactly hang out with billionaires. I wouldn't know what to say, and I'm very sure I have nothing to wear. God…" Her face began to grow pink. "I can't even imagine consorting with your family. No. Not gonna happen. Give them my apologies."

"Ha!" Seth laughed. "You're a snob!"

That brought her head up. She glared at him.

"You are."

"I am not," she argued indignantly.

"Yes, you are. Snobbery goes both ways. You think you're too good to eat a simple meal with my family. In my book, that's a snob."

"That's not at all what I said! You're turning it around."

"So prove me wrong. It's going to be a barbecue at the ranch. Jeans and boots. Probably finger foods. If you're not too good for that, then prove it by coming."

She looked at him then, her eyes filled with unshed tears.

"Seth, you know what I'm saying. I would be a laughingstock."

He reached out and took her gently by the shoulders, turning her to face him. "No, you wouldn't. If you'll just meet them, I think you'll find they are a laid-back, fun-loving bunch who will treat you with complete respect. I guarantee within fifteen minutes, you'll feel like part of the family."

"And why would I want to do that?" she asked, shrugging out of his arms. "How am I supposed to sit and make conversation with these people knowing all the time I'm a fraud? Knowing all the time they're the sons of the man who caused me to lose my farm. Maybe that doesn't bother you, but it bothers the hell out of me."

"First of all, I don't believe my brothers had anything to do with taking your ranch. Secondly, you're not a fraud. We are married. The marriage certificate is on file at the courthouse, and the ring is on your finger."

"Yeah, but for how long?"

"How long does anyone have, Ally?" he shot back. "There is no guarantee in this life."

"You're twisting my words again."

"No, I'm not. Dammit, Ally." He pulled her to him, and his lips came down over hers.

At her resistance, he immediately loosened his hold, but when she didn't move away, he continued the kiss, his arms going around her. One hand moved up to her head as he held her to him. "Open your lips for me," he growled against her mouth. When she complied, he covered her lips with his, his tongue going deep, searching and discovering her hidden secrets. He heard a soft moan, and his body surged to full attention. He felt her hands slide up his chest and over his shoulders.

He broke the kiss and nuzzled her ear, inhaling the natural sweet perfume of her body. He looked down into her face. She was standing with her eyes closed, her lips open and waiting for him to return. Sexual urges raced through his body, and he took her mouth again, this time not so gently. He was on fire, and he wanted her in the worst way.

He felt her hands against his chest, gently pushing him back. Reluctantly he lifted his head and stepped back.

"I… I'm sorry," she whispered. "I can't do this."

She turned and walked to the barn. This time he let her go.

# Six

That evening Ally accompanied Seth back to the hotel, where they gathered their things and Seth checked out. This was it. The day she'd dreaded. She and Seth would live together under the same roof. It had seemed different living at the hotel. But this…moving into the house…was very real.

She had been an idiot to let him kiss her. Not that she could have done anything to prevent it. Down deep where no one would see, she had wanted his lips on hers since that first day they'd met at the crossing of the road and the bridle path. Then with each successive encounter, her desire for him had grown. If she were honest, part of the reason she so dreaded him living with her in this house was because he was the kind of man who could undermine her defenses.

No woman was immune to those eyes…those lips. He had an aura about him that worked like a magnet, drawing a woman into his web.

But she had to be strong. This was a temporary situation, and in a few months, he would be gone. She didn't intend to be left with a broken heart when she saw him off, but if she wasn't careful, Seth was just the man who could do it.

It had bothered her when Wayne Burris left a year ago, more than she cared to admit. She knew when they began a relationship that Wayne was biding his time until he put some money together to get back on the rodeo circuit. That was his life. Anything or anyone he met along his journey eventually became a forgotten memory. Like a fool she thought she would be different; she would be the one he couldn't leave. She would be the love of his life and he'd want to stay and make a home together. It had hurt when she found the note on her pillow. By the time she awoke and read it, Wayne was long gone, never to be heard from again.

Seth was the same way. She didn't have any proof but she knew. He was a billionaire, a jet-setter who traveled places she would never see. The women in his life were fun times along the way, there temporarily but soon to be forgotten. She wouldn't let herself be a fool this time. The marriage certificate changed nothing. And she didn't intend to go through abandonment again. Seth was pure temptation. But there was always a price to pay for indulging in the kind of temptation he represented.

That evening as Ally dressed for bed, she couldn't stop thinking about Seth. It felt both strange and oddly comforting to have him here with her. She got in bed determined to stop thinking of the handsome man. She could hear him moving around in the room next door, the old floor creaking with every step he took. She heard the shower come on. A few minutes later, he turned it off. She heard him as he walked to his bed and got in. Apparently they didn't believe in insulation in these old houses. She was surprised she didn't remember hearing sounds when she lived here before. But then, her dad had stayed in the extra room downstairs, unable to easily navigate the stairs. Maybe that was why.

The old house popped and squeaked, and it seemed the darker the night became, the more sounds she could hear. Finally she drifted into a restless sleep.

The sound that woke her came from downstairs. She immediately sat up in the bed. Not moving, she listened closely for another crash. She was sure that's what had woken her up. What could have fallen? It sounded like someone was in the house, prowling around the kitchen. She inhaled deeply.

*You're being ridiculous.*

The only way to know for sure was to get up and go down there. She swung her feet to the floor and stood from the bed. About the time she opened her bedroom door, another crash came from downstairs. Maybe it was Seth getting a glass of water. But he would turn on a light. Wouldn't he?

Her heart was beating hard in her chest as she turned in the direction of the stairs. Seth's bedroom door opened, and she heard him call her name. She ran back to where he stood in the doorway of his bedroom. He was shirtless, and his hair was in disarray. The moonlight highlighted the muscles in his arms and stomach.

"Ally? What is it?"

"There…there was a crash downstairs. Twice. Were you just downstairs getting a glass of water?"

"No." The door opened wider, and he pulled her into his room. He quickly put on a pair of jeans and, opening a bedside drawer, picked up a large-caliber handgun. After checking the load, he slipped it into the back of his jeans. "Stay in here."

He walked through the open doorway, and Ally was right behind him.

Seth stopped, and she bumped into his back.

"Ally." He kept his voice low. "Stay in the bedroom."

"Not happening! What if someone is down there?"

"Then I'll take care of it. I don't need to worry about you getting in between us."

He turned her around and gave a light push toward his bedroom before he disappeared into the deep shadows of the hallway. She reached his door, but before she could step over the threshold, she heard another sound coming from downstairs. The temptation to follow Seth was strong. But instead she backed up and closed the door. Making her way to his bed, she sat down on the edge and clasped her hands tightly together.

Maybe she should call the police? No, she decided. She had lived here her entire life and had never experienced any sort of break-in. The very idea was preposterous.

Time seemed to crawl by. About the time she'd reached the end of her patience, Seth walked back into the bedroom.

"We had a break-in," he told her, his voice conveying annoyance. "Someone was looking for something and apparently tripped over the boxes that were still on the kitchen floor. About the time I turned on the lights, the back door slammed behind him. I got to the door immediately, but he was already gone, disappeared into the night."

"We should call the police," she said as she headed for the door.

"I already have," he responded as she bolted toward the door. "Where are you going?"

"Downstairs. I want to see what damage they did. How dare anyone break into this house!"

"Ally, I didn't see any damage. Wait until the sheriff gets here."

"You wait if you want to," she retorted as she rushed from the room, Seth right on her heels.

The kitchen was a mangled mess of open cabinet doors and drawers pulled out and dumped on the floor. The few remaining boxes were scattered around as though someone had kicked them out of their way.

A few minutes later, they heard a siren getting closer. Seth answered the knock on the front door and led the deputy into the kitchen, where together they made a full report. Mason Crawley, the deputy sheriff, painstakingly wrote down all the facts, but without a description of the man, there was little he could do. He would put out the word and send extra patrols throughout the night.

As soon as he was gone, Ally set about closing all the cabinet doors and putting back the drawers. After restacking the boxes with Seth's help, she rubbed her arms and looked for something else to do.

"Come on, Ally," he said stepping up behind her, crossing his arms over her shoulders and around her neck, holding her close. "Let's see if we can get some sleep. There's nothing more we can do in here tonight. I doubt if the burglar will be back. I'll arrange to have some security here tomorrow."

She solemnly nodded her head, and together they walked up the stairs.

"I want you to sleep in my room."

"No, I'll be fine."

"I'm not willing to take the chance," he countered and guided her to the master bedroom.

She let him help her into bed before he went around to the other side and placed the gun on the nightstand. He slipped in between the sheets and turned off the light.

"Who would break into the house?" she had to ask, still sitting up. "They must have seen the cars and known someone was living here."

"I'm guessing somebody was squatting in the house during the months it sat vacant. They probably left something important and are desperate to get it back. I suggest we go through the house thoroughly tomorrow and see if we can find anything you don't recognize."

"Absolutely. Seth?"

"What, sweetheart?"

"I'm glad you were here." She felt a shiver go down her spine. She would have gone downstairs herself and encountered no telling what kind of situation.

"Come here," he said as his arm went beneath her and he pulled her close.

"I just wish I knew who it was."

"Let it go for tonight, Ally. Maybe the sheriff's office will find who did it."

"Or maybe they will come back."

"You're safe, Ally." He pressed her head down onto his shoulder. "Try and go to sleep."

"I'm not worried about my safety. I want to catch the creeps. Ugh! I feel so violated. How dare anybody break into this house! If you're right about it being a squatter then they will be back. But we haven't found anything unusual in all the cleaning that's been done recently. Still, I intend to go over every inch of the house tomorrow."

"And I'll help you. But for tonight you really do need to let it go. Get some rest."

She shrugged. "You're right. It's just that I've never experienced a break-in before."

"I left the downstairs lights on for tonight."

"You don't think he'll come back, do you?"

"Doubtful. Between me catching him inside and the police coming I seriously doubt if he'll try anything else. At least not tonight."

Ally willed herself to relax. It felt good to have Seth's warmness surrounding her. Being held tight and feeling protected wasn't something she was accustomed to, but she couldn't deny the comfort it gave her. Tomorrow…tomorrow she intended to go over this house until she discovered what would draw someone into the house even knowing someone was at home. With one last sigh of determination, she turned into Seth's neck and, breathing in his essence, closed her eyes.

After dressing the next morning, she went downstairs. Seth was sitting at the new kitchen table, sipping a mug of coffee and reading the local newspaper. She helped herself to a cup and sat down across from him.

"How'd you sleep?" he asked without lowering the paper.

"Good. You?"

"Like a rock. There's something about this country air that just intensifies everything." He put down the paper and looked at her. "The breeze is cooler, the air crisper, the scents of the clover and wildflowers more fragrant. And this old house…you can sense the culture, like it's steeped in tradition. And that's saying nothing about my sleeping partner." He looked at her and grinned. "Yep. Definitely slept like a rock."

"I guess." She shrugged, ignoring his sexual jibe. "It was an old house when Dad bought it. He had a lot of updates done but insisted on honoring the integrity of the original." She stretched and stifled a yawn. "Well, I'm headed to the barn. The stalls are mostly cleaned, but some other things need to be done. Then I'm coming back and with the household staff I'm going to turn over every nook and cranny in this house."

"I'll walk with you."

He stood and poured the remains of his coffee into the sink. Then together they walked the path to the stable area. Once inside, she grabbed a rake and began mucking out one of the stalls that still needed some cleaning, trying her best to ignore Seth. Every time he came near her, she felt herself heat up. It soon proved difficult to focus.

"Explain to me why you won't have dinner at my brothers' ranch."

"I already did."

"They're nice, laid-back people, Ally. Chance is a rancher, same as you."

"Somehow I doubt that." She cast a skeptical look in Seth's direction.

"Maybe he has a bigger spread, but he is a rancher. Other than a stint in the navy, it's all he's ever wanted to do. His wife, Holly, is a veterinarian. Her clinic is across the road from the ranch. You remind me of her in a lot of ways. Cole is the businessman of the bunch. Has an office in Dallas, but they choose to live on the ranch. He commutes into Dallas a couple of times a week. His wife is an archaeologist."

"An archaeologist?"

"That's right. In fact, they met when she obtained a court order to search a section of the ranch for artifacts. They originally hit it off like oil and water but eventually got together and have been in love ever since. Wade is the newest married, besides us. He used to spend most of his time in Europe, but since he met Laurel, he has pretty much delegated the work to someone else. I've never met her, but I understand she is an accomplished artist. Other than some stray cousins, that's the family. And they all want to meet you."

Ally kept sweeping at the debris in the stall. She didn't know how to answer him. Here stood the man responsible for getting her ranch back wanting to introduce her to the men arguably responsible for taking it away. To Seth this was a small thing he was asking of her. She supposed she owed him this much. But how she could feign being a happily married bride for an entire evening, answering questions and making small talk? Especially with the entire clan of Masters brothers and their wives?

She sighed. "All right. I'll go. But I have to go to town and find something to wear."

"Not a problem. We'll go tomorrow."

She stopped raking. "No. *I* will go. I'm quite capable of buying my own clothes." She looked at Seth and saw him nod. She needed some new clothes anyway. She might as well take advantage of this excuse and take the time to buy some. She'd use the money she'd been saving for breeding fees and hope she could earn it back before it was needed. She wasn't about to appear at a barbecue at the home of a Masters in worn out jeans and a raggedy T-shirt.

By Saturday all of the repairs on the barn had been completed. The last of the supplies for the house had been delivered, and her horses were scheduled to come back to her stable on Monday. Everything should be in order, but the evening's festivities still loomed. Ally didn't want to go to the Masters ranch and visit with Seth's brothers and their wives. Still, she'd promised Seth she would go.

At least she had plenty of outfit options after her shopping trip the other day. She'd bought a whimsical pale green blouse and denim skirt with wedges to match, plus two other dresses just in case. It had felt good to be out on a full-blown shopping excursion. She hadn't done that since Wayne Burris had dumped her for the rodeo circuit, leaving a note that said he hoped she would understand. Oh, she'd understood, all right. Macho males seemed destined to sweep in, make a woman feel special then in the blink of an eye disappear again, never to return. Wayne had been popular with the ladies and knew how he affected them. He'd expected Ally to understand that, too.

She went inside the house in search of Seth. She found him in an extra bedroom with one of the ranch hands, arranging a new desk, chairs and filing cabinets. He'd decided he needed a home office, and she couldn't think of a reason to deny him.

The ranch hand immediately nodded and excused himself.

"So what gives?"

"My new office. Do you like it?"

"Oh, yeah. It's…an office."

"I've made arrangements to fly in two of my security detail."

"You have a security detail?"

"Yes. A necessary evil, I'm afraid. Anyway, they will stay a couple of weeks and help the sheriff's office find the person who broke in. Once they arrive, they'll have rotating shifts overnight. I don't want any more surprises. I doubt you do, either."

Ally shook her head. "Pauline and I looked everywhere and found nothing that could belong to a squatter."

"Maybe there's nothing to find," Seth said.

"I intend to keep looking. Your office does look good, though," Ally said, changing the subject. "Where will your assistant sit?"

"Hopefully I won't need one locally. I guess I'll cross that bridge when I get to it."

The day passed quickly. Too soon it was time to get ready for the evening outing. After a hot soak in the tub, she dried her hair and donned the new blouse and skirt she'd purchased. With a light touch of makeup and some lipstick, she was ready to go.

Seth stood waiting for her at the front door when she came down the stairs.

"Very nice."

"Thanks. Let's get this over with."

She didn't miss the grin that sprang to his lips. She wished she was as calm as he appeared. He opened the door. "After you."

She walked to the truck, where Seth helped her inside then they were on their way.

# Seven

It was a twenty-minute drive to the ranch, and Seth felt Ally's anxiety the entire way. But he knew once she really got to know his brothers and their wives, she would be at ease. He wished she didn't have such preconceived concepts of his brothers, but he could understand where they came from after her history with the Masters family, particularly his father.

She looked incredibly beautiful, the pale green blouse accentuating the deep auburn highlights of her hair and the emerald green of her eyes. A touch of pink lipstick made her full lips irresistible. Kissing. They needed kissing.

Seth turned off the main road and drove under the metal Masters Ranch sign arching over the wide drive. They passed the original house on the left. The sprawling stone-and-log structure was a vision set against the backdrop of the deep pine woods. They continued along the drive, past the main barn capable of housing one hundred horses. Its white columns and dark green facade spoke to the quality of the Masters breeding program that had long been heralded by local ranchers. They then turned off to the west. The road curved around rock formations and deep blue pools then went up a rise until Chance's house came into view. Similar to the original house though not as large, it was still breathtaking. Seth felt Ally's uneasiness heighten.

"This is it," he said. "This is where Chance and Holly live."

He parked the truck behind another and helped her out.

His brothers were awaiting their arrival in the front yard. They each embraced Seth, and he proceeded to introduce them to Ally.

"Glad you could come," Chance said. "Come around to the backyard and make yourselves at home. We're eating outside tonight."

"Welcome! It's so nice to meet you," said a beautiful blonde woman as Ally rounded the corner of the large house. She came forward and hugged Ally. "I'm Holly. This is Laurel and Tallie," she added, pointing out the two women who now joined them. They each grinned and welcomed Ally to the group. "Dinner is almost ready. Burgers and steaks. Hope you like pecan pie and homemade ice cream. Martha is our cook. She's making her mother's recipe for dessert."

Soon everyone was seated around the large table on the stone patio. The area was edged by a rail fence that looked out over the grasslands nestled between the higher elevations with the river running like a ribbon through it all.

As the time passed, Seth watched Ally begin to engage in the banter with the other wives. That she was ill at ease was clear, but eventually the other wives worked their magic and Ally began to respond. Soon she was laughing at the stories of how each couple got together.

"What about you?" Tallie asked.

"Seth almost ran me down with his car. Had to jump the hood to keep from becoming roadkill."

"Oh my gosh! What is it about these Masters men?" Laurel shook her head.

"Hey, now." Wade spoke up. "It isn't entirely our fault."

"Nope. It sure isn't," Cole chimed in. "We're the ones caught off guard. It's the women who cause all the friction."

"Friction?" Laurel and Holly both repeated.

"I'll remember that, bud." Tallie glared playfully at her husband, her eyes sparkling in challenge.

"I want to propose a toast." Holly spoke up, raising her glass. "Here's to our husbands. May they all reap what they sow."

"Hear, hear," said Tallie. The others raised their glasses.

Ally joined in the toast, but Seth caught her glance as she did. Underneath the smile was sadness. He was sure of it. She hid it well, but in that instant he had seen through her bravado. Was it knowing theirs was only a marriage of convenience, and of short duration at that? He frowned. She'd assured him she didn't want any long-term commitment when he first approached her about this arrangement, so it must be something else.

When it was time to leave, the group saw them out to the truck. On the way home, Ally was quiet.

"So, what do you think of my family?"

"They're all great," she replied. "I really enjoyed tonight, Seth. Thank you."

"My pleasure."

"You were right. They weren't the awful people I had imagined. I still don't understand what really went on between my father and yours, but I accept your brothers had nothing to do with it."

"I honestly can't see Wade or Cole or Chance doing something like that. I'm sorry if my father caused you unnecessary pain."

Out of the corner of his eye, he saw her shrug.

"It's a beautiful night," he continued.

"Yes, it is. I loved the view from the terrace where we ate dinner. You said all your brothers have homes at the ranch?"

"Yes, they do. Wade and Cole have to make trips into Dallas periodically, but they told me they're all happier at the ranch."

"I can understand that. I wouldn't want to be anywhere else. I mean, if it were a choice between the city and the country."

"I never minded the city, although I grew up there and didn't know any better. I must admit, the country is starting to grow on me." He couldn't help grinning. "I want a horse."

"I'll put the word out that you're looking. Do you want a specific breed?"

"Whatever you recommend."

"You might also call Chance. He could probably fix you up with the perfect mount. The Masters Ranch carries some of the best bloodlines in the country. If I'm remembering correctly, they have several different breeds."

"Why don't I arrange a day for us to go and see some? Have you ever been inside their barn?"

"No, and I would love to see it."

He glanced over and saw her smile. "Then consider it done."

Soon they pulled into the long driveway going to the house. Seth walked around to her side of the truck and helped her out. As her feet touched the ground, he held her just a moment longer than he probably should, but she made no move to walk away. The moonlight glistened on the strands of her hair, turning them to a burnished gold. His hands moved from her shoulders to cup her face, and without giving it a second thought he lowered his lips to hers.

He heard her inhale deeply before she opened her lips to his. His arms came around her and pulled her tight against his body. The taste of her made his hunger increase, and like a starving man, he fed. Her mouth was a deep well of temptation, and he couldn't get enough. He heard her moan, and his erection throbbed inside his jeans.

"Let's go inside." His voice was rough even to his own ears.

Suddenly Ally pushed against his shoulders and stepped away from him. "I… I can't do this. I'm sorry, Seth."

"What's wrong?"

"You're bored and I'm here. I've played that game before, and I won't do it again."

She hurried to the front steps. He looked up at the dark sky then rubbed the back of his neck. Maybe she was right. It wouldn't last. She knew that and so did he. His only excuse was that she was impossibly tempting.

He followed her inside the house and to the kitchen. She was there, taking a glass from the cabinet. A glass of water sounded good.

"Do you mind handing me one?"

"Sure," she replied, giving him a glass and walking to the faucet.

"Did someone hurt you?" he couldn't help but ask.

She took a sip of her water and was quiet for a long moment. He didn't think she was going to answer. But then she said, "His name was Wayne. Wayne Burris. We were together a few months. Long enough for him to make promises. Plenty of time for me to fall for him and believe what he said. The next thing I knew, I found a note on my pillow. He said he hoped I would understand. No problem there. It was never his intention to stay around, but I let my hopes get the best of me. I was a fool. But I'm not about to put myself in that situation again. God, I hate that man. He goes through his life not caring who he hurts, not giving a second thought to the people he interacts with. The world revolves around Wayne."

"It doesn't have to be like that."

"No? Then how would you imagine this will end? Eventually you'll leave to go back to California and that will be that."

"I'll be back, Ally."

"You can't say that, Seth. If there's one thing I've learned, it's that the future is never set. You want an affair, and I'm saying no."

"I can't promise anything more right now. Why don't we take it one step at a time and see where this goes? I think you're attracted to me a lot more than you want to admit."

"You're crazy." She turned away and headed for the den. He caught up in four long strides, stopping her forward progress and turning her back to him. His hands cupped her face.

"Don't judge every man by one man's bad behavior."

"I'm not. I—I'm not."

"Yes, you are."

With lips set in determination, she pulled free and continued her flight to the stairs.

Ally finished off the last of her eggs, took a bite of toast and walked to the sink, rinsing the crumbs down the drain. The morning was overcast, dark clouds on the horizon telling of rain in the distance. She hoped the rain would hold off. While they needed a good downpour, there were too many things to be done that required dry weather.

Seth started a fresh pot of coffee. It smelled like a lifeline, and she eagerly grabbed a mug from the cabinet and poured her second cup.

"So, what time do your horses arrive?" he asked.

"All I know is before noon. Mac Dempsey, the manager over at the Triple Bar Ranch, is bringing them himself this morning. He said he would try to be here by noon."

"Good deal. I'm happy for you."

She looked over at Seth. "You know what? I think I'll take my coffee to the barn. I need to get out there early." She walked to the kitchen door and stepped out onto the covered porch where she'd left her boots. Pulling them on, she slipped outside without a backward glance.

An hour later the van arrived holding Ally's three mares and her stallion, Monkey.

The ranch hands were there to assist in unloading them from the trailer and into their stalls. Hay was provided and plenty of fresh water.

When they were all settled and happily munching on their hay, Ally turned to Mac.

"I can never thank you enough."

"Glad to do it. They're beautiful, quality mares. I'm glad they could come home again. It's where they belong."

Ally hugged the older man, tears forming in her

eyes at the remembrance of all he had done for her after she lost the ranch. "Thank you so much."

She stepped back just as Seth entered the barn.

"Mac, this is my husband, Seth. Seth, this is Mac Dempsey."

The two men shook hands. "You two have a fine place here," Mac said, putting his hat back on. "I guess I don't have to tell you, but you're married to one of the best trainers in the state. I'm glad she's home, but we're sure going to miss her."

"I understand," Seth replied. He looked at Ally and grinned. "She's pretty special, all right."

Together they walked Mac out to his rig and saw him off. Then Ally hurried back inside the barn. Stopping at the first stall, she sprang the latch and stepped inside, pouring the morning grain into the feeding trough. Seth came in and stood in the entrance to the stall.

"This is Lady Mary, a thoroughbred out of Nimbus Cloud Rising," she said as she ran her hands over the horse's chest and down her legs. "She has produced some of the finest foals around. I'm going to try to save up and breed her to Standing Tall Vision, a stallion out at the East Fork Ranch."

"Why not mate her with your own stallion?"

"He's her son out of Jault Amar. Standing Tall Vision is currently a high-stakes winner in the major races. Don't know if I can do it by next year, but I intend to try. His stud fee is several thousand dollars, but a colt out of the two of them would be unprecedented."

She patted the mare's shoulder and backed out of the stall, closing the latch behind her.

"This is Sassy Lady," Ally said, dipping up another measure of feed and going into the next stall. "She's a quarter horse." The mare was a bay with one white foot and a blaze face. Slowly Ally approached the mare and ran her hands over the legs and back.

"Is she in your breeding program, too?" Seth asked.

"Yeah, but I'd rather wait and make Lady Mary the priority. I can't afford the breeding fee on them all, and the foal Mary produces will sell for enough to pay the breeding expenses for both of the others and then some."

She fed the third mare, a chestnut with three white socks, then stepped across the wide hall to where her stallion stood, patiently munching his hay.

"This is my Monkey man, also known as Jupiter's Rising Star." She ran her hands over the horse's glistening black coat after pouring the mixture of grain into his feeder.

"He's a fine-looking stallion," Seth commented.

"He's a thoroughbred. He's produced four colts, and they all did great on the racetrack. I've had quite a few inquiries about him already, but Mac didn't have the room to set up a separate area for breeding. That and his barn is full, so no way to board any mares." As she talked the stallion turned to her, searching her jeans pockets for a treat.

"Hey, there, Monkey. I've got your carrot right here."

She pulled two carrots from her back jeans pocket, and he eagerly snapped them up.

"Why do you call him Monkey?"

"When he was a yearling, he was into everything. His antics almost took him out more than once. But the crowning glory was when, at two years old, he became enamored with two mares a couple of runs down. Mr. Monkey here decided he would just jump the fence. And he did. He went sailing over a six-foot-high expanse of pipe fencing. But while his front feet cleared the top rail, unfortunately his hind feet didn't follow and he hung himself on the top rail. His front feet were swinging about an inch above the ground and his hind legs were straight up in the air. Quite the sight. Mac was over visiting Dad and he came running. He sized up the situation and pushed Monkey's hind legs up and over the top rail. Monkey landed in a heap, bruised but thankfully otherwise unharmed. Mac called him a crazy monkey, and the name kinda stuck."

Seth laughed. It was the first time she had heard such a bellow of laughter from him. She grinned.

"He loves carrots but won't touch apple slices or corn. Most horses love all of them. Monkey spits out a piece of apple as quick as it goes into his mouth."

She turned to Seth. "Thank you for making this happen, for allowing me the opportunity to bring them all home."

"Not a problem. Glad to do it. Don't forget, this ranch was only part of the arrangement. You made funding for the research center possible."

"Well, I'd better get back to the house. I want to do a full search. See if I can find whatever that thief was looking for."

"My two security staff should be arriving this afternoon. I need to have a meeting with them," Seth said. "I would help you, but I have no idea what I'm looking for."

"That's okay. Neither do I, really. But I think I'll know it if I see it."

They returned to the house together, then Seth got in his truck to drive to the local airport to pick up the men.

Ally went to the kitchen to try her search again. She pulled out each drawer and went through the contents and examined the bottom. When she finished with that room, she headed to the living room then on to the den. Pauline joined her in the search for a while, then went back to cleaning upstairs.

By the time Seth returned from the airport, Ally had nothing to show for her efforts except a list of grocery items she needed to pick up at the store. It was a long list. And if she knew Seth at all, he would insist on going with her. She'd never been around anyone who wanted to protect her like he did. He was a special man. She just had to be sure to protect her heart as well. It was becoming more difficult every day.

"Guys, this is my wife, Ally," Seth said when he found her in the den. He stepped aside so his security men could enter the room.

"Nice to meet you," she replied and shook their hands.

"Frank, I want you to stay around the back and cover the west end of the house tonight. Bryan, you take the front and the east side."

The men nodded.

"I don't know what to tell you to look for. I don't have a clue what the guy was doing inside this house. But if he comes back, I want him caught. There are two spare bedrooms on the left side of the hall upstairs. Make yourselves comfortable. T-shirt and jeans will work here and help you blend in with the ranch hands. You're welcome to roam around the property and get your bearings. I suggest if you run into any of the ranch hands, you introduce yourselves as friends of mine here visiting for a few days. Word travels fast around here, and I don't want news of a security team getting back to the culprit. And try to get some sleep. You're on duty at ten o'clock."

"Yes, sir," both said in unison.

"I'll show you to your rooms," Ally offered and walked toward the stairs. The housekeeper stood at the top of the stairs.

"Pauline, these are friends of my husband, Frank and Bryan. This is Pauline, our housekeeper." Ally led them to the upstairs hallway and continued on to the guest rooms. "I think you'll be comfortable. If you need extra blankets, check the closet. Anything else, Seth and I will be around, or if we aren't, Pauline should be able to help you."

"This is great," said Bryan, stepping inside one of the rooms. "Thanks, Mrs. Masters."

Seth stepped up behind where the small group stood. "Any questions?"

"Is there any outside security?"

Seth shook his head. "No, not yet. I prefer to wait and see if he tries something else before we go full-scale surveillance. That could draw attention and scare him off. I want this creep caught."

"We're on it," Frank advised.

Seth turned toward Ally. "I'll drive you to town if you need to go to the store."

She gave him a tight smile and headed for the stairs.

In the kitchen they faced off in the argument he knew was coming.

"I'm fully capable of driving myself to town," she said, her hands on her hips.

"I know that. But what I don't know is who broke into this house last night—or why. He could have been after you."

"What? That's ludicrous."

"Maybe. But I'm not willing to take a chance. You're welcome to go with one of the security team instead of me, but I'd prefer you not go into town alone."

"Fine. Let's go. This time. And Seth?"

"Yeah?"

"Don't do this again."

# Eight

Seth drove the seven miles into town and parked in the lot of MacKenzie's grocery store. Ally was out of the truck and hurrying toward the front entrance by the time he rounded the vehicle. She grabbed a shopping cart and headed for the vegetable aisle. She picked up some lettuce and potatoes before walking around the corner to the next aisle. When Seth arrived she was talking to a tall man who was reaching out for her. Ally's body language said she was anything but pleased to see him. Each time he reached out to her, she backed away. Seth stepped up next to her, and she seemed to relax at his presence.

"Seth, meet Wayne Burris," she said, stepping closer to Seth. "Wayne, my husband, Seth Masters."

"Masters?" he repeated, showing his surprise.

"Well you did real good for yourself, darlin'." He offered his hand to Seth, who reluctantly shook it. If his memory served, this was the man who'd walked out on Ally, leaving her to face her father's death and the loss of the ranch alone.

"So, how long have you been married?"

"A few weeks," Seth answered. He brought his arm up around Ally's shoulders and kissed her on the cheek.

"Newlyweds. Well, all right." Wayne scratched his jaw, looking thoughtful. "You guys living out at the Masters Ranch?"

"It's been nice to meet you, but we've got to get going," Seth told the man, ignoring his question and leading Ally away toward the meat counter.

"Yeah, you too."

Ally was visibly shaken. It must have been a shock to see her ex again, seemingly out of the blue. Had there ever been love between them? Did she still have feelings for the man?

She finished her shopping without saying a word and headed to the checkout. Seth paid the bill and accompanied her back to the truck. She didn't wait for the store employee to finish loading the groceries into the back before she opened the door and got in. Seth climbed in after her.

"Are you okay?" he asked before starting the engine.

"Yes, I'm fine. I just never expected to see him again."

"Ally, is that the guy you were telling me about?"

"Yes."

"Are you in love with him?" he asked quietly.

"No," she immediately responded. "I question if I ever was. How can you love someone when he's never around? He hit on half the women in this town before I found out about it."

Seth started the truck and backed out of the parking space. He was glad he'd insisted on coming along with Ally. There was just something about the man he didn't like, other than the obvious.

"Again, thank you for being there, Seth."

"Not a problem."

Ally was quiet on the drive home. The housekeeper bustled out and helped bring in the groceries. Ally looked lost. Clearly it had something to do with meeting Wayne Burris.

Suddenly she turned toward Seth. "Are you up for a ride this afternoon?"

"I would be if I had something to ride."

"You have three very well-trained mares to choose from. I'd like to see the property and double-check the fences. Thought it might a good outing."

Seth grinned. "Sounds like a plan."

By two o'clock Ally had saddled the chestnut and bay mares and they were on their way. Seth was impressed by his horse's training. They let themselves through the large back gate and headed north. The recent snow had melted and the trees were showing their tiny buds of spring. Though still early in the year, the sun was shining down and the sky was a clear blue.

They rode through open pastureland then followed a trail into the trees until they eventually came to a small lake surrounded by large boulders. Ally dismounted and led her mount to the edge, where it splashed in the water. Seth followed, and they let the horses drink. Ally took a canteen from her saddle and offered it to Seth.

"How many acres do you have here?" he asked, handing the canteen back to Ally.

"Almost five hundred, but as you can see, not all of it is suitable for grazing. There's a lot of timber. Still, it's enough. I prefer to do hands-on with the horses I get in for training so I never have more than a dozen here at any one time."

"They do training at my family's ranch, too."

"As I understand it, the Masters Ranch has several trainers and a manager that oversees their breeding program. Then there are the cattle. It's a magnificent operation."

"It's big," Seth added. "As kids we never thought about the size and all that went on. We had chores, but once those were done, we were off searching for some adventure that most likely would land us in trouble." He chuckled. "Good memories."

Ally tied her reins to a nearby tree limb and climbed to the top of a boulder that overlooked a spot where the river flowed into the small lake. Seth followed suit.

"This used to be my favorite place. Dad always knew if he couldn't find me around the barn or house, this is where I'd be."

"Your thinking place."

"Yeah. When I was little, nothing seemed as bad up here. Problems had a way of disappearing for a while."

"Speaking of problems," Seth ventured. "I'm going to need to go back to LA for a couple of days. Something has come up with the research center sooner than I expected. I want you to come with me. I have a place right on the beach. I think you'll enjoy it."

"I don't know... There are so many things I need to do here. I'm barely moved in and—"

"And it will still be here when we get back. You have a housekeeper to oversee the house and four good cowboys to take care of the horses and any other ranching issues that may come up. Past that, there are now two security men to keep an eye on things. Frankly, security or not, I don't want to leave you here until they find whoever tried to break into your house. Granted, my security team is good, but there is always room for mistakes. I don't want to take the chance."

"What would I do in California?"

"What can't you do in California?" he countered and grinned. "It's only for a couple of days. Come with me. Let me take you out to my favorite restaurants, show you the places that are special to me like this place is to you."

Ally looked again at Seth. He seemed to hold the world in his hands. So strong and capable. It had been years since she'd taken any time off. Doubt and worry had plagued her ever since her father had gotten sick and died and the ranch had gone into foreclosure. Having a few days to cast her worries aside sounded almost too good to be true. If she had any sense at all, she would just thank Seth and accept his generous offer without questioning if there was an ulterior motive. Seth was not Wayne. And although it was hard to let go of the grip of caution she'd always carried, she wanted to trust Seth.

"Okay. I'll go," she told him. "Thanks for the invitation."

"You're welcome. If you have nothing in particular keeping you here, we'll head out in the morning. My plane is fueled and standing by at the local airport."

He had a plane? Oh, of course he had a plane. Probably more than one.

"Do you like what you do?" It was a question that begged asking. She loved working with the horses, but Seth was on a completely different playing field. If she made a mistake, it might mean a sprained wrist or loss of a week's work. If Seth made a mistake, it could cost millions, and that pain would have to be a good deal worse.

"Yes," he answered. "My businesses are diversified enough that it isn't the same thing week after week. I get to meet new and interesting people, go interesting places. And I'll probably be doing even more traveling once everything is in place and I officially join Masters International as a working partner. I'll have not only my own companies to oversee but new assignments with the family corporation as well."

"It's not going to leave you much downtime."

Seth's intense brown eyes held hers for a moment. "No, it's not."

He'd be here one day, gone the next, with no end in sight. At least he wouldn't have to worry about leaving a family behind. He and Wayne were alike in that way. Always anxious to see what lay around the next bend or just over the far hill. Relying on quick wit and skill to achieve their goals. Risk takers. Full speed ahead.

The thought made her sad.

They climbed back in the saddle and veered east, following the fence line. Over the next rise, they saw where a large tree had fallen, landing on top of the fence. Ally made note of the location and they continued on. Eventually the sun began to set and they turned toward home. The cowboys were waiting on them to return and kindly took the reins. Each horse would receive a good brush down and their nightly feeding. And she and Seth would return to their own rooms. Another day would have passed. Then a new assignment would take Seth away. Tomorrow, it would be Burbank. After that, the world.

The private jet was ready for takeoff when they arrived at the airport at seven the next morning. Ally couldn't believe how luxurious the main cabin was as she took her seat next to Seth and buckled her seat belt. Within a matter of minutes, she was watching the world grow smaller as the plane shot into the cloudy sky. Breakfast was served by a flight attendant, and in under two hours they were circling the airport in Burbank, ready to land.

A limo was waiting to pick them up in front of a small avionics hanger near the private landing strip. Everywhere Ally looked, there were palm trees and flowers. The sky was bright blue, dotted here and there with wispy white clouds. It was as different as you could get from the still brown landscape of home.

Once their luggage had been transferred and they'd settled into the back seat of the limo—which was larger than her cottage on the Triple Bar—they were off, turning onto a busy road with more palm trees, flowers and blooming hedges edging the highway.

"It's beautiful here," she said, staring out her window. Before Seth could answer, his cell began to ring. He spent the rest of the trip in conversation with one person or another. Eventually the limo pulled up under a large portico, and the driver walked around the car and opened the door. Ally stood up and waited for Seth. He ended his call and accompanied her past the building's security and into a waiting elevator. At the top floor, a soft ding announced they had arrived, and the doors silently swooshed open. They stepped out into a foyer decorated with a mixture of potted plants and ferns.

"Good morning, Mr. Masters," said a uniformed servant. "Welcome home."

"Good morning, Brewster." Turning to Ally, he added, "this is my wife, Ally."

"Of course." Brewster smiled.

With fluid precision, the houseman opened another door and stepped aside to let Ally and Seth enter. It was a world she'd only seen in magazine articles about the wealthiest people in the world. The main living area was open, the room as big as her entire barn, with a view of the Pacific Ocean framed by floor-to-ceiling glass panels.

"Put Mrs. Masters's luggage in my suite," Seth instructed, watching Ally for a reaction. "Ally, I have to go downtown for a short meeting. Make yourself at home. The kitchen is through there. If you don't find what you want, ask Brewster. Order anything you want. Feel free to wander. I'll be back as soon as I can. Promise."

He stepped up to her and slowly pressed his lips to hers. "I'm sorry to drop you off and leave. I'll make it up to you tomorrow."

"I'll be fine. Don't hurry on my account."

He kissed her once again, this time with more passion. Too soon he broke it off.

"Derrick?" he called out.

"I'm here, Seth," a tall, imposing man replied as he stepped into the room.

"Derrick, I'd like you to meet my wife, Ally. Ally, this is my head of security, Derrick Johnson. He'll accompany you wherever you want to go. The car is available if you'd like to see the local sights or do some shopping. The beach is just a few steps from here. Just tell Derrick and he will make sure to set up anything you need."

"Oh, well… I'll be fine here until you get back…" she said and swallowed hard. "Sweetheart," she added, not knowing how to address Seth in front of other people. It seemed to tickle Seth. With one last kiss, he walked out the door, closing it behind him.

Derrick handed her a cell. "This is a phone with a pager. Just push the red button and I'll be here as quickly as possible."

"Okay, and please, call me Ally."

"Let me know if you need anything, Ally." And with a polite nod he disappeared into the foyer.

*Holy crap.* She couldn't get her head around this. She walked to the far side of the room and opened the sliding glass doors to the large balcony. The ocean was a blend of dark blues and turquoise. A few beachcombers walked along the edge of the incoming waves. Colorful umbrellas dotted the sand as far as she could see. It was as different from the pasturelands of Texas as one could get. Still, as beautiful as it was, a longing for home surged through her.

Seth was back by seven o'clock that evening and seemed happy to see her. She was definitely glad to see him. He was her link to home and despite her denial she was ready to head back. She met him at the door with a hug, which seemed to surprise them both.

"What did you do with your day?" he asked, removing his tie and jacket.

"I sunbathed out on your balcony and watched the ocean. It was nice."

"Good. You need some downtime."

"Well, I sure got some today. I almost fell asleep," she grinned at him.

Seth smiled back. "Ally, the good folks who are involved in the research center want to have a gathering tomorrow night at one of the local hotels. Nothing big, just cocktails and hors d'oeuvres. I really want you to go and meet the people. I've arranged for Karen to take you shopping tomorrow while I'm at the office. I thought you might like a new dress for the occasion. She knows the stores and said she would be delighted."

"That's very nice but I don't need to go shopping." She didn't know what to say. She didn't have the money for an expensive dress she would only wear once. Panic began to work its way up her spine.

Seth must have noticed her reaction. He came over to her and cupped her face in his hands.

"Ally, if it's about money, please don't worry about it. I want to do this. I want you at the party. I want to introduce you to everyone there. I don't care if you wear jeans, but I thought you would feel more comfortable wearing a cocktail dress. That's usually what the other ladies wear to these things."

She took a step back and his hands fell to his sides. "Introduce me as what? An old friend from Texas? A casual acquaintance? An associate? You surely can't introduce me as your wife."

"Why not? That's what you are."

"That's ridiculous."

Seth bit on his lower lip, then continued. "Ally, it would mean a lot to me if you would attend…as my wife. No one has to know our marriage is temporary or the reason for it. I can always explain that it didn't work out at the end of the three months."

Hearing him say those words made her sad. It shouldn't have, but it did. Seth approached her again, this time lowering his lips to hers.

"You are a very beautiful woman," he murmured against her lips. "Go shopping with Karen. You'll like her. Have a good time. See some of the sights that I won't have time to show you. Buy a dress. Buy ten."

"Attending a special event was not part of our bargain."

"It's part of being my wife. We have to keep up appearances here as well as in Texas. Because of the center, there will be reporters asking questions and taking pictures. I guess you should prepare yourself for that, too."

"But—"

"I want to kiss you." He saw her eyes fall to his lips and he couldn't stop from placing his mouth against hers.

It started as an innocent kiss but immediately the tenderness and warmth turned it into something more. Seth raised his head and looked at her expression. Her eyes were closed, her face upturned toward his. He kissed her again, and this time she couldn't help but respond. Feeling that response, Seth immediately deepened the kiss. She felt his arms go around her as his lips moved to her ear then down her neck. "Or if you don't want to go shopping, I can think of something else a husband and wife could do."

He raised his head and watched her as confusion filled her. At times like this it was as though Seth was treating her like a real wife, like theirs was a real marriage. She didn't know what to make of it. Or how to respond.

"All right. I'll go. But your bank account will be sorry, and I make no promises to repay you."

He laughed. "None needed. What shall we do for dinner?"

# Nine

"Do you like Italian food? Or seafood? What's your favorite?"

"I rarely get great seafood."

"Okay." Seth grinned. "There's a new seafood restaurant in Malibu I have yet to try. It's getting rave reviews. Does that sound like something you might like?"

"Sure," she said, looking down at her jeans and boots. "Can I have a minute to change?"

"It's casual." Seth indicated his own attire. "But, of course, take all the time you need."

She ventured down the hall where she'd seen Brewster take their luggage earlier. At the end were double doors to what must be the master suite. When she stepped inside, her jaw dropped. The high ceilings and painted-linen walls gave the room an airy, spacious feeling. Three arches led out to another terrace that provided exquisite views of the sea. And she couldn't help but notice the bed, fit for the master. With its brown, blue and off-white bedding, it was masculine yet very luxurious.

Ally roamed through the massive expanse until she came to another set of double doors. They opened to a walk-in closet filled with suits and shirts and casual clothes. In a smaller section to the right, someone had hung the dresses and blouses she'd brought with her. She stepped forward and selected a navy blue dress and matching sandals.

Through still another door was the powder room and bathroom with floor-to-ceiling mirrors and a hot tub that would easily hold six. Across the room a rain-forest shower with ferns and an assortment of foliage tempted her. But the shower would have to wait. The small bit of makeup she'd brought was laid out by the sink along with her hairbrush and other toiletries. She quickly brushed her teeth, freshened her mascara and lipstick, and declared herself ready to go.

Soon they were on their way to the Sand and Sea. The restaurant was repurposed from an old distillery perched on the edge of a cliff that overlooked a lighthouse and the ocean below. Seagulls flew overhead, occasionally dipping low toward the water. The scents of salt water and cedar filled the air around them.

A tall man with a ready grin pushed open the

rustic door and welcomed Ally and Seth. "Mr. and Mrs. Masters, your table is ready," he said and led the way across the room to a table by the window looking out on the water. The soft illumination of a single candle added an enticing glow to the darkness around them.

"How does he know who we are?" she whispered to Seth.

"Does it really matter? He might have seen my face before, and I told him our name when I made the reservations."

"You mean he's seen you on the news or in the papers, don't you?" To be recognized in public like that must mean Seth had quite a high profile.

"Come on, Ally. I've heard the lobster here is truly delicious."

"I don't care for lobster," she snapped.

Seth gave her that grin that would no doubt melt any female heart. But not hers. She felt slammed into this unreal world, off balance and totally unprepared for what might come next. When Seth had asked her to accompany him to California, she'd thought… well, she *hadn't* thought it would be like this, and she was not prepared for such luxury, such opulence. She didn't like feeling off-kilter, and to make it worse, Seth knew it and was laughing at her although he tried to hide it.

"So, how did your meeting go?" Ally asked after they had placed their orders.

"Good." He smiled. "Groundbreaking is set for early June. How was your afternoon?"

"Okay. I found a spot out on your balcony and watched the boats and the people. I especially loved the surfers. What must it be like to have your back door open out onto the ocean? Do you go jogging in the mornings?"

"Actually, I did for a while. Then the business started to really grow and there was less time every day. Then I was spending fewer days here in the States, which made it even harder."

"You really should make time for jogging again. The mornings are the best. You can lose yourself. Clear your head and make plans for the coming day."

"Is that what you do?" He draped his linen napkin over his lap.

"When I go riding? Yes. I usually take one of the horses on a brisk ride just as the sun is coming up. They seem to like it as well."

"So that's what you were doing the day we…met."

"Yep." She picked up her glass of ice water. "And you cratered my whole day."

Seth reared back and gave a husky laugh. "Now I understand why you were so upset."

"Well, yeah. Almost being run down."

"Seth!" A woman's voice came from behind her. "I thought that was you!"

As the woman approached their table, Ally looked into her laughing blue eyes. She was a tall brunette, model thin, who made no effort to disguise she was enamored with Seth.

"Gayle." Seth acknowledged her and stood from his seat.

She stepped into his arms and kissed him on the cheek then looked up into his eyes as if expecting him to do or say something more. *Hello? Don't mind me*, Ally thought.

While Ally knew she had no right to be jealous, she couldn't stop the sensations of anger and resentment that began gnawing at her stomach. Before she could take another breath, Seth set the woman away from him.

"I want you to meet my wife."

The woman's head shot around, and she looked at Ally in surprise.

"Ally, this is Gayle Honeycutt. Her father and I have done a lot of business together. Gayle, my wife, Ally."

"You're married?" the woman gasped. She looked as though she'd just been slapped. But she gathered her wits quickly and produced a smile that would challenge anyone who would accuse her of not being happy for the new couple.

"Congratulations," she breathed. "Oh my gosh. You didn't let us know you were getting married." She turned toward Ally. "Are you from this area?"

"Texas."

"Texas? Really. Well, he certainly kept you hidden."

"Hidden from what?" Ally managed to give the woman a blank stare.

"All the ladies whose hearts will now be broken." She eyed Ally with suspicion. "I would love to know how you reeled this one in. We've been trying for years."

"Gayle." There was a warning in Seth's tone.

That seemed to bring her polite facade back up. "I'm just saying. Well, nice meeting you, Ally, and good luck. Seth, take care."

"You too."

She disappeared as quickly as she'd appeared, into the darkness of the low-lit restaurant.

"Sorry about that." Seth returned to his seat.

"Oh, no. No apology needed. This is your hometown, and it would surprise me more if you didn't have women clamoring over you. I'm just sorry you had to share our secret."

"You mean our marriage?"

"Yeah. It's going to cause a rift in your social life when you come back after the three months are over."

"Don't worry about it." He flexed his jaw as if he were agitated.

The appetizers were served, and for a while the conversation stilled, but it wasn't an uncomfortable silence. The shrimp cocktail was delicious, as were the salad and homemade bread. The wine he'd ordered tasted incredible with the food. Ally forgot her nervousness and let herself enjoy the dinner. She had just laid down her fork after a delicious main course when the waitress came back to check and make sure everything had been okay. When dessert was offered, she turned it down. She couldn't hold another bite. She and Seth ordered coffee to finish out the meal.

"This was delicious. Thank you, Seth."

"My pleasure. I enjoyed it as well. We'll have to come back again sometime."

Ally smiled. Seth might come back, but it wouldn't be with her. In two days they were due to return home. Ally was ready. This break in her daily routine was nice, but her place was in Texas. It was where she fit. What she knew.

"Seth Masters, you sneaky thing!" Another woman approached the table. Seth muttered something foul and politely stood up.

"Rachael," he said.

"I just ran into Gayle Honeycutt…this is your wife?"

"Ah, yes. This is Ally. Ally, meet Rachael Larson."

"Nice to meet you."

"I can't believe you're married," this new woman said, turning back to Seth. "You never let on you were seeing someone seriously."

"Now you know," Seth told her and returned to his seat.

"I guess so." She eyed Ally then returned her gaze to Seth. "Well, good luck to you both."

"Thanks, Rachael."

He looked at Ally. "Are you ready to go?"

"Yes."

Without another word, he stood from the table and reached for her hand to help her up. They headed for the door.

* * *

Seth couldn't believe his luck. Two women he'd once dated showing up at his table within an hour of each other was unbelievable. He could only imagine the impact it had on Ally. But then again, why should it? They weren't in love. They had not married under normal circumstances, so why should he worry about the effect this had on her? He helped her into the car and walked to the other side and got in.

"I'm really sorry about that, Ally."

"About what?"

"Gayle and Rachael showing up like that."

She shrugged. "It doesn't matter to me. Why should it? We're not really married, plus I never assumed you'd been a monk."

"Good."

Ally turned her head and looked at him, one eyebrow going up.

"I mean it's good you weren't bothered by them showing up."

"Not at all. So, we leave the day after tomorrow?"

"Two more days. Think you can stand it?"

"It'll be good to be home again."

Seth was still grimacing as they walked through the door to his condo. He'd asked Ally to accompany him to California to show her a bit of his world. But that didn't mean she'd sleep with him in his bed. She'd no doubt have major objections to sleeping in his suite. With him. And he couldn't blame her.

While he was majorly attracted to Ally, he sensed her pulling away from him.

"Would you care to take a late-night stroll on the beach?" he asked as they crossed the threshold. "It's a full moon, and usually on nights like this there's plenty of light."

She stood still, contemplating her answer. "I'd like that."

Moments later they were standing at the condo's private entrance to the beach. Ally slipped off her shoes. Seth did the same.

"It's been a long time since I did this, visited the ocean. Especially at night. My work has become increasingly hectic. When I'm home, I rarely notice the ocean anymore. Even the view."

"That's too bad. You need to find some time to enjoy this. Especially living seaside. You must love the beach to want to live here."

"Yeah, you're right," he answered as they stepped out onto the sand. It felt both flour-soft and crisp at the same time. Somewhere in the night, the seagulls called to one another away from the sound of the waves rolling onto the shore. The moon cast its light down over the water, highlighting the spray of each wave. A soft breeze filled the air.

"It's beautiful," Ally commented. "I can smell the sea."

He watched as she ran to the edge of the water and laughed as the waves rolled over her bare feet. "It's warm! Come on, Seth. Be daring." She laughed and held out her hand to him.

He approached her and took her hand. Together they began to stroll down the beach.

"We have beaches in Texas, but the sand isn't this soft. I used to go with some friends back when I was in school. I loved the ocean," Ally said.

"We have that in common. Growing up I used to walk along the shore and look for things the tide had brought up. I had a whole treasure trove of driftwood and dried starfish. My mother finally threw up her hands at me bringing so much trash, as she called it, into the house. But I thought it was special."

"Do you still have your collection?"

"Nah. After she died I sold the house, and my treasures had to go."

"That's too bad. I would have liked to see some pieces."

He'd never told anyone about his love of beach-combing. People would probably laugh it off as a childhood phase. It suddenly hit him that he hadn't hesitated in telling Ally. Somehow he knew she would understand.

"What did you like doing as a kid? Any child-hood fascinations?"

"Antiquing. The land on the ranch is riddled with artifacts from both the Native American culture and the Civil War era. I once found a set of eyeglasses and a small metal powder flask used by a soldier. I've found clay pots and arrowheads and a piece of jewelry. I still have most of my finds, but for me, the fun was in the looking."

Seth grinned to himself. "Definitely."

Ally stopped and bent down, retrieving something from the sand.

"What did you find?"

"Just a piece of shell. I would think it would be fascinating to walk along this beach during the daytime."

"It is. Especially early in the morning when the tide is going out. You can find lots of shells and all sorts of stuff. We will have to make time to do just that the next trip in. This is a private stretch of beach, so not a lot of people get to the treasures."

Ally was quiet for a long time. As they continued their walk, he had to wonder what she was thinking.

"What's the matter, Ally?"

"Not a thing. Just that this has been a great mini vacation. I haven't once worried about the horses or break-ins or anything that might be going on at the ranch. I owe you a huge amount of gratitude for taking me away from all the worries for a while."

"Not a problem. We will have to do it again."

"You know that isn't going to happen. You have your life and I have mine. Even if you didn't mind carrying around the extra baggage, I have responsibilities. Anyway, by the time you need to return to California, our time together will probably be over."

"It doesn't have to be," he said, stopping in his tracks, pulling her to a halt.

"Yes, it does."

"Why? Tell me why."

He didn't wait for her answer. He pulled her into his arms and found her lips with his. She was soft and welcoming, her scent standing out as pure, luscious desire against the aroma of the sea. He heard her moan, and his desire doubled. He pulled her body firmly against his, wanting to show her what she did to him. Her arms climbed up and over his shoulders, and she ran her fingers through the short hair at his nape. She was so responsive, so sensual, he knew the possibility existed that this would get out of hand fast and he would take her right here on the beach.

Pulling back, he cupped her face with his hand while bestowing kisses on her cheek and ear.

"I want you," he said. "There's something between us. I know you can feel it, too. Let's go back to the condo."

She studied his face in the moonlight. Finally she nodded in agreement, and his excitement surged. He had to kiss her one more time. It started in gentleness like the soothing waves that crept up on the shore: calming, relaxing, providing a glimpse of what deeper waters held in store. But the underlying power of a storm that pulled an ocean to the brink of fury settled between them, and he knew there was only one way to silence the turbulence.

He released her face and took her hand and began the trek back to his penthouse. The warm waves rolled over their feet but he hardly noticed; he felt like the air had been torn from his lungs. All he knew was Ally. All he wanted was Ally. It wasn't supposed to be like this. He never intended their marriage to be consummated. But there was something about her he hadn't known with any other woman. There was no comparison. There was no right or wrong. There were no second guesses. He would have her.

# Ten

He pulled her into his arms again as soon as the elevator doors closed. She was hot and trembling and oh so decadent. He pushed her into the corner, lost in the moment, his mind leaving his body to be replaced by pure animal instinct.

The doors opened, and they were inside his condo. Her shoes fell to the floor as he swung her up and into his arms and walked purposefully toward the master bedroom. There, next to the bed, he set her on her feet and began taking off her dress.

Again his lips found hers in the inky blackness of the night. He knew the passion that lay between them was only a breath away. She could deny it all she wanted, but he could taste it, feel it. Smell the arousal on her skin. She wanted him as much as he wanted her. He couldn't promise her forever. He couldn't promise anyone that. But he could give her now.

For long moments she kissed him with raw, honest emotion, giving back each kiss, each stroke of the tongue. Her hands moved to his chest, and he wanted her touch on his skin. Ripping open his shirt, he placed her hands against him. Cupping her hips he pulled her to him, pressing his erection against her belly. He felt her shudder. He pushed her hair back from her face and kissed her jaw and neck and nuzzled her ear before moving to the other side. He heard her moan and felt her hands go around his back, pulling him closer.

Ally felt as though she was in a dream. She knew what was coming. It both excited and terrified her. She didn't want to have feelings for this man. But he was under her skin, and she knew tonight she wouldn't say no again. She stood watching him silently as he undressed her; the soft blue dress fell silently to the floor, followed by her bra. His mouth formed a thin, tight line as he concentrated on what he was doing. She reached out to his belt, unhooking it, then found the button on his jeans.

"Let me help you, sweetheart." His voice was raspy, deep. Her heart beat a fast rhythm in her chest as he quickly unzipped his jeans.

Then he again picked her up, laid her softly on the bed and followed her down. She had never made love with a man she had known less than three weeks, but that thought didn't linger. Seth had shown up in her life and turned her world upside down. He wasn't like any other man she had ever known or would ever know.

She cupped his face in her hands, feeling the texture of his five o'clock shadow. Her thumb played against his full lips, and she felt the grooves on either side of his mouth. The world grew more intense. He smelled like the robust cologne he wore mixed with his own unique manly scent. His body was hot, aroused. It served to bring her own body to a highly awakened state. With gentle kisses he sent adrenaline zipping down her spine. He nibbled at her neck, and she threw back her head to allow him more access. His hands played with and molded her breasts, then his lips trailed down and he licked in circles around each nipple. She moaned with need.

"What is it, Ally?" he whispered in a deep, masculine voice. "What do you need?"

"Please," she whispered.

"This?" he asked playfully, running his tongue over her pink nubs.

"Yes," she said and arched her back.

"Or how about this?" he murmured, taking one bud between his lips and sucking gently.

She was on fire. She strove to breathe as she clutched the hair at his nape.

"I need to be inside you," he said, taking her other nipple in his mouth and giving it the same treatment. "Are you ready for me?"

She felt him reach down between their bodies and test the wetness between her legs. Two fingers probed the opening then pushed gently inside. Her body naturally squeezed, increasing the need she had for him as her legs spread wide. He pushed her gently back on the bed, removing her bikini panties as he hovered over her, sliding them down her long legs.

He straddled her on the bed, one leg on either side, holding himself above her with his arms. She felt his erection at the entrance to her womb. Raising her knees, she moved to where she needed him to be. He entered her then, slowly, then withdrew before entering her once again. Deeper this time until she felt his rhythm and sought to hold on and move with him.

"God, Ally," he rasped. Then with one hard push, he was fully inside. She inhaled deeply, sharply, at the full penetration.

"Easy, sweetheart," he said in her ear. "Just take it slow. God, you feel amazing."

Ally couldn't speak, couldn't think. She was lifted off the bed by pure sensation that wrapped her from her head to her toes. She thought it couldn't get better. Then Seth began to move again. Slowly at first, drawing back and pushing increasingly deeper with every thrust. She found herself on the edge of a great precipice, and only Seth could determine whether she shot to the heavens or rode the wave that seemed to go on forever.

She sensed his forearms on either side of the pillow, his hands under her head as his lips again found hers. His tongue entered her mouth and filled her before withdrawing. He emitted a low growl, biting at her lips and throat. Pushing into her. It was raw sex. Unlike anything she had ever experienced.

He slid his fingers through her hair and held her head as he feasted on her lips, her mouth. Then he was biting her ear, sucking her lobe, his breathing hot and rapid. His hands again cupped her breasts, pinching the swollen buds, and a current shot from her chest to between her legs. He pushed in deep, his hips rotating. The world stood still.

"Come for me, Ally." It was a hot demand, his voice rough and guttural.

Her body complied. Without warning, she was caught up in the whirlwind Seth had created, soaring toward the stars and feeling as though she would never come down. Her breath surged from her lungs, and she didn't care if it ever came back. She felt him push hard over and over, deep into her, before calling out her name as he joined her in their shared ecstasy.

Seth fell to one side and hugged her close to his body. Breathing hard, he pressed fevered kisses against her brow, her cheek, her lips.

"Are you okay?" he asked, his voice still low, still winded.

She nodded. "Yes." In fact, she was better than she'd been in a long time. For these few remarkable minutes, the burden she carried dissolved into nothingness. She snuggled into his strong arms and inhaled his arousing scent. She felt safe and protected, and even though her conscious mind knew it was just for the moment, she let herself enjoy the sensation. Sleep overtook her as she settled into his arms.

* * *

The next morning Ally stretched and yawned. Drawing in a deep breath, she opened her eyes. Something was off. This was not her room. She sensed warmth next to her, and immediately the events of the previous night flooded her mind. Turning her head, she came face-to-face with Seth's twinkling eyes.

"Good morning," he murmured sleepily. "Sleep well?" He grinned, leaned over and kissed her.

"I did. Too well." She stretched and felt unfamiliar discomfort between her legs.

"Did I hurt you?" he asked, looking deep into her eyes.

She felt a blush run up her neck. "No."

Seth had made love to her again during the night, and as stupid as it was, she hadn't denied him. She knew she was asking for trouble down the line. The day would come when she got used to being with him. And fast on the heels of that would be the day he said goodbye. It was inevitable. He was a globe-trotting executive who had no intention of settling down.

What had she done? She'd made love to Seth Masters, that's what. And she had never been loved as deeply and as thoroughly as she had last night. She'd been right. Seth Masters was amazing in bed. So much so that she didn't regret one instant. The ecstasy had overwhelmed her so completely it took away any regrets she might have otherwise felt this morning.

But she wouldn't fall in love with him. She absolutely wouldn't. She wouldn't be that foolish. Again. Making love with Seth so far overwhelmed anything she'd felt with Wayne, it wasn't even a contest. Who was this stranger who had dropped into her world and turned it inside out and upside down?

She stretched again, slipped out of the bed and headed to the shower. The soothing spray was exactly what she needed. For a few minutes, she claimed the right to indulge in its heavenly warmth. Eventually, her hands getting pruny, she stepped out of the shower. After drying off, she wrapped a towel around herself and returned to the suite to get dressed.

Seth wasn't there. She supposed he was using another shower in the apartment. She toweled her hair dry and combed it out before getting dressed. When she was done putting on her makeup, she stepped out into the hallway.

"Good morning," Seth said from behind her. She turned around. He was looking way too sexy in a white bathrobe as he strolled into the main room. He walked over to her and lifted her chin with his finger. Bending over, he placed his lips against hers, and Ally felt the sizzle of temptation run throughout her body. "The coffee should be ready, and there are fresh pastries on the counter," he said against her lips. "Make yourself at home while I get dressed."

She grabbed a cup of coffee and a croissant and went outside, finding a seat on the terrace. The morning activity made the beach a different place than it was last night. People were talking and laughing, and there was music playing somewhere in the distance. It wasn't long before Seth joined her, walking just past where she sat to stand at the balcony railing.

He turned to look at her. "I have a conference call today, around ten, and I have to be at my office for that. Karen should be here about the same time to pick you up."

"Then I'd better go get dressed."

Karen Silverton arrived at exactly ten o'clock. A perky blonde, she was not at all what Ally had expected. Welcoming and warm, she introduced herself, and they were off. Karen was a genuinely nice person who gave Ally the lowdown on what to expect at the types of dinner parties and social events Seth attended. Ally didn't bother to tell her this was a one-shot affair.

Over the next couple hours, they went to innumerable shops, and the dresses Ally tried on were elegant and stylish and made her feel like she'd just won the lottery. Whether red or black or gray, each fit her to perfection. She especially liked one of three-toned brown, starting with gold at the neck, with the layers of fabric getting darker as they fell to her knees. It felt elegant and took away any hint someone might have that she was a cowgirl.

They had lunch at a small restaurant in Hollywood. Karen was easy to talk to and commented several times on how much she enjoyed working for Seth.

"He's a real guy," Karen said. "No arrogance, no games. Just straightforward and honest. In the seven years I've known him, he's always maintained that he would never get married. Imagine my surprise when he told me he'd done just that. You are one lucky lady, if you don't mind me saying so. Of course, Seth is lucky, too. I'll bet you made a beautiful bride."

Ally smiled and swallowed hard. Only she and Seth knew there was no bride, no engagement. Just a sham marriage of convenience. She realized she was in over her head with this arrangement. For the first time since accepting Seth's business proposal, she wished she'd said no. She'd imagined a wedding, of course, but then the two of them would pretty much go their separate ways. The very last thing she'd thought would happen was that she'd be sharing a house with him and becoming part of his life. Now she was lying to his administrative assistant. And Seth, the honorable man Karen thought him to be, was lying, too. Somehow Ally felt as if the entire charade was her fault.

"The clothes will be delivered in the morning," Karen explained as they got in the car to head back to the condo. "Saves us carrying all those bags."

Ally felt bad about spending so much money on clothes. At least she would happily wear them. They wouldn't sit idle in her closet. It was the first truthful thing she'd done since marrying Seth and it felt good.

Ally spent the afternoon getting ready for the research center reception. She had chosen to wear a dark violet cocktail dress with tiny sequins sewn into the material. It set off her hair and her slim figure. She looked amazing. Beautiful. She'd had a manicure, and her make-up set off her high cheekbones and the delicate features of her face.

The limo was there on time, and they were off.

When she and Seth walked through the door to the hotel restaurant, all eyes turned to them. Rather, to Ally. Cameras flashed as several partygoers came forward to greet Seth and introduce themselves to Ally. Her grin ever at the ready, she shook their hands and returned their compliments as though she'd been doing it her entire life. She seemed perfectly at ease and was immediately accepted by various people in the group.

"It's certainly nice to meet you, Mr. Smothers. And is this your beautiful wife?"

"It is. Ally, meet Gretchen," the older man replied, and his wife stepped forward to shake Ally's hand.

"Your dress is lovely," Mrs. Smothers said. "It goes so beautifully with your hair."

"Well, thank you. That's very kind of you to say." Her southern accent stole the show. "And thank you for your kind contribution to the treatment center."

Seth watched as Ally made her way around the room, talking to the people, laughing, accepting a drink from one man, compliments from several. He felt pride as he watched her work the crowd. He tried to keep up but was pulled aside by a few attendees who didn't realize this was supposed to be a celebration, not a business meeting.

Later Seth caught up with her at the punch bowl.

"My feet are killing me," she said through a smile. "How much longer are we expected to stay?"

"Not much longer. You've handled this beautifully, by the way."

"The people are nice. It's easy to be nice back. But you'd better watch Larry Buddress. I thought I was going to have to kick his leg. He latched on and wouldn't leave me alone."

"He came on to you?" Seth was horrified.

"No, but he flattered me to no end. Only because I'm your wife. He's a climber. Wants to get to the top of your group and figured buttering me up was the way to get it done faster. I just really hate people like that. Oh. Look out. The man himself is headed this way. This time he's all yours. I've gotta find a ladies' room. Later."

Seth turned to find Larry approaching them, his hand out.

"Larry, good to see you. Thanks for coming," Seth said.

While the man went on about all the things he could do for the project, Seth saw Ally turn down a hallway and walk out of sight. Just before she turned the corner, he saw her take off her shoes and couldn't help but laugh.

The music started, and he walked over to where Ally had disappeared. Soon she came back down the hallway, still holding her shoes.

"Put your shoes on and dance with me," Seth said, humor lacing his words.

"Ugh."

When she put them on, he took her hand and led her to the dance floor. The small orchestra was playing a slow song, and he pulled her into his arms. It felt good to hold her. She fit his body perfectly, and they swayed to the music, his arms locked around her, pulling her close. Her head lay against his shoulder.

The music changed to another slow tune, and they continued to hold each other as they swayed to the beat. Ally didn't say anything and neither did he. Being close was enough. No one tried to cut in. It was as if they knew she was his and interruptions would not be tolerated.

The evening was winding down. When the music ended, Seth led Ally back through the crowd, and they began saying their goodbyes. As they made their way toward the door, several men stepped forward and patted Seth on the back, congratulating him on marrying such a fine wife.

Seth felt good about the research center. So many people had come forward pledging their help and making donations. Within two years they should be close to opening. He wouldn't have been this close to making it happen if it weren't for Ally. He wished he could tell everyone about what she had done to help the project along, but of course he couldn't. As far as everyone knew, they were a happily married couple.

Until their three months were over.

"Are you asleep?" he asked, looking at her as she lay back against the leather seat of the limo, her eyes closed.

"No. Just thinking back over the party. The people were so nice. Are they all going to contribute to your project?"

"Most already have, and others have made pledges."

"I'm so happy for you. Your dream is going to come true."

"Yep. Thanks to you."

"I've done very little. You're the one who made it happen."

"On the contrary, the building itself will cost several million dollars. The proceeds from my father's will are going to cover most of that. There would be no inheritance were it not for you."

"You're sweet to say that."

"I imagine you're ready to get back to the ranch."

"What time will we leave tomorrow?"

"I have another meeting in the morning. I should be back by noon then we'll go. You can sleep in."

"It's been great, Seth. The entire trip. You live in a very beautiful part of the world."

He smiled. "So do you." And he meant it. He hoped she would return here someday, but there was no use inviting her to come back. They both knew that probably wouldn't happen. She had her life in Texas, and he had his in LA. Maybe a visit was possible if life didn't get in the way. But he was about to start his role in the family business in addition to maintaining his own companies and working on the research center. There was no use kidding himself.

When this was over, it was over.

# Eleven

Ally didn't want to leave LA. For perhaps the first time in her life, she didn't miss the ranch. Being here with Seth had been a wonderful experience. Last night had been so much more than she'd ever dreamed. Dancing in his strong arms, feeling his body sway to the music, alternately pushing against her then stepping away. By the time they'd left the party, she was so hot she'd practically attacked him as soon as they made it through the door of his condo. Then they'd fallen into each other's arms and the evening had exploded into pure ecstasy.

She'd better lock it away in her memory book, because it wouldn't happen again. It couldn't.

Now it was time to go home. Seth was back from his meeting by one o'clock, and they were on their way back to Texas. The flight was quick by comparison to their trip out to California, when she'd been on pins and needles. Seth hadn't mentioned anything last night to indicate any change in his feelings, but he looked at her in a different way—a twinkle in his eyes and a look of possession on his face. Like she was his.

It wasn't true. It never would be. But just for the moment, she let herself believe it was. Just for the moment, they were husband and wife and the life they led was real. A warm feeling began to grow as she remembered all he'd done for her. He didn't have to. He'd gone over and above, and she'd begun to see him as someone special. The chemistry between them came alive whenever she was with him, and now it was strengthened by the love that had started growing in her heart.

She shook her head to remember none of it was true. None of it was real. She could savor being in Seth's arms for now. But when the plane touched down, all fantasies were off.

Ally had been quiet this morning, and Seth didn't try to encourage her to speak, deciding to let her work through it in her own way. He wished, however, he knew what she was thinking. Had he taken advantage of her? She'd given no indication she regretted last night. So all he could do was assume it had been as incredible for her as it had for him.

The small town of Calico Springs came into view as the plane circled for final landing. Seth looked over at Ally, surprised to find her dozing lightly. He couldn't resist leaning over and placing a kiss on her succulent lips.

"Mmm," she murmured, opening her eyes.

"We're here. Time to wake up."

She blinked as though recalling where she was. "Okay." She smiled up at him, and his body surged with want. God, she was a beauty. Her crystal-green eyes sparkled, while her full lips parted in a smile, showing perfect white teeth. Framing her delicate features was that dark red hair laced with strands of burnished gold from the sun. Her small turned-up nose completed the effect.

He looked forward to being at the ranch once again. Enjoying some alone time with Ally. First thing on his to-do list was to find a horse of his own. He'd call Chance and see if they could come out and look at any he had for sale. Then they could go exploring and share a day.

"Did you ever hear anything from your security team about the break-in?" Ally asked, sitting up in her seat and straightening her clothes.

"Nothing. All was quiet while we were away."

"Good. I'd hoped they would catch him, but quiet is good, too."

"If the person thought the house was empty, he no doubt had quite the surprise. It might take him a while to get up the nerve to try again. But we're ready for him."

"Good."

"Ally, how about I call Chance and see if they have any horses for sale?"

"Great idea."

"Or maybe we could borrow a couple of their horses and make a day of it on my family's ranch?"

"I would like that. I've heard it has some of the greatest views of anywhere around. And you can ride for days."

"I'll call Chance tomorrow morning."

Once they landed, they made the trip from the airport to the ranch in silence. Entering the house, Seth noted it felt as though he was returning home. In the few weeks he'd lived here, he had come to regard it as home away from home. Bryan from his security detail met them at the door.

While Seth stopped to talk with Bryan, Ally continued up the stairs to her room. He hoped her interludes of silence weren't indicative of something wrong.

It was good to be home again. The days spent in California had been good, especially the time spent with Seth, but home was nice, too.

As Ally stepped inside her bedroom, she noted the room felt out of sync. Everything was the same but felt different. She set her luggage on the bed and sat down next to it.

What would happen now that they were back? Recent events had changed everything. Could they return to the way things were? She felt a kind of panic at the thought. It would be no use pretending that they hadn't made love. But how did they go forward from here? She was trying hard to keep barriers in place that would prevent her from falling in love with Seth, and he probably had barriers equally strong that kept him free and able to live his single lifestyle, unburdened by any relationship that would tie him down. Where did he see their immediate future? She knew he was as determined to maintain his freedom long-term as she was to maintain hers.

She never should have made love to Seth. But she had, and while she didn't regret it, she was in the dark about where it put them going forward. Did she talk to him about it? Or just keep quiet and play it by ear?

That seemed to be the best alternative. The only trouble was she wanted to make love to him again. That didn't mean she had to fall in love with him. It didn't mean he would lose his freedom. Did it?

She stood and opened her suitcase. Taking her clothes out of the bag and hanging them in the closet kept her hands busy but couldn't stop her mind from wandering. She was glad he'd gotten his inheritance. She was thrilled she got her ranch. She should just stick to thinking about that and leave the relationship alone. Trouble was, it was easier said than done.

She changed into her jeans and a loose shirt and headed to the barn. It was late, but she wanted to check on the horses. As soon as she stepped inside, the familiar scents of alfalfa, molasses and leather filled her nostrils.

"I had a feeling I would find you here," Seth said

from behind her. He put his hands on her shoulders, turning her around to face him. "Is everything all right?"

"Yeah, it appears to be." She looked over at the stalls. The horses had finished their grain and moved on to munching on their hay. They looked contented and happy.

"Good. I have to make some phone calls. It will keep me tied up for a while, in case you wondered where I was."

"Okay. Thanks for letting me know. I guess I'll see you in the morning."

"No. You'll see me later." He gave her a devilish grin before he turned and walked out of the barn.

Ally fiddled with the horses for a while then, realizing she was tired, turned off the lights and walked toward the house. Seth hadn't said anything about their trip to LA. She should have felt relieved, but she didn't. He probably wasn't giving it two thoughts, which only made her yearn for the closeness they'd discovered. Apparently it meant a lot more to her then it did to him.

When she got back to the house, she decided to get ready for bed. The shower felt good. It reminded her of the rain-forest shower at Seth's home. She got into bed and turned off the bedside light. She needed to put this past weekend out of her mind. Stop dwelling on it. The house grew quiet, and she finally drifted off into a restless sleep.

In a fog, she felt lips against hers, reminding her of Seth's kisses. As sleep receded, she became aware that it was Seth kissing her. She couldn't stop her moan of welcome. The kiss deepened, and his arms came to rest on both sides of her, cradling her face, playing with the strands of her hair.

"Did you finish your phone calls?" she asked when he raised his head.

"All finished." He nuzzled her neck, making shivers go down her spine.

"That didn't take too long."

"Mmm. It's two o'clock, Ally. You've been asleep for hours."

"Does your work always require so much of your time?"

"Yes. Unfortunately."

And his job would always come first. Yet another reason why she must maintain a friendship and not fall in love with Seth Masters. Even if he cut back on his work, which wasn't likely, there was no future with him. She would not again fall for a handsome man knowing only too well all the future held was another note on her pillow.

"I want to make love to you." His deep, throaty voice threatened to overcome her determination to put some space between them. Her body reacted to his words as if she had no control at all. A rush of pure fire ran down her spine, and she fought to hold still and not press herself against him.

"I… I don't think that's a good idea."

"Oh? Ally—"

She pushed him back and struggled to sit up.

"I let it get out of hand in California. We shouldn't

have made love. We've taken our relationship to the next level. This can only end badly."

"It doesn't have to."

"But it always does."

Seth was quiet for a long time. Long enough that Ally began to regret her words. Yet she couldn't take them back. They were true. And if this relationship grew deeper, she would be the one who suffered when he said goodbye.

"Okay," he said finally. "I'll see you tomorrow. Sleep well."

She doubted she'd be able to do that.

He stood from the bed and walked to the door. "Good night, Ally." He looked back at her one more time before closing the door behind him.

What was she doing? Was she crazy? Apparently Seth wanted her as much as she wanted him, and she'd just rejected him. He probably thought she was some kind of tease.

With that unsettling thought, she rolled onto her stomach and bunched the pillow under her head. It was going to be a long night.

By five o'clock she was no closer to a sound sleep than when she'd first lain down. The covers were oppressive, but when she kicked out from under them the room was too cold. Memories of being with Seth filled her mind. The walk on the beach. The restaurant. Kissing him at the water's edge with the sound of the ocean all around them. Making love…

Those women.

This wasn't going to work. There would be no

more sleep tonight. All her body wanted was to be touched by him again. To feel his big hands roaming over her, squeezing her breasts, to feel the nips on her neck causing electric currents to race over her body.

Frustrated, Ally sat up in the bed. Seth was next door. Did she dare wake him up? No. That would only increase her need for him. She moaned to herself and punched the pillow. It was, indeed, going to be a long night.

The sun had yet to reach the horizon when Seth dressed and headed downstairs. He paused in the kitchen to make a pot of coffee before going outside to find Bryan. The night had been quiet—too quiet, in more ways than one. But the intruder hadn't come back. It had been two weeks, and there hadn't been any more incidents. He would talk to Ally later when she woke up and see what she thought about sending his security guys back to California. He didn't want to make the decision without her input. Perhaps she still needed the extra assurance right now.

After talking with Bryan, he headed back to the house. The eastern sky was a soft pink as the sun began to crest over the horizon. As he entered the kitchen, he was surprised to find Ally helping herself to the coffee. She looked tired, worn-out, not her usual perky self. He had to wonder if her night had been as restless as his. It couldn't be. At least not for the same reason. He had tossed and turned through the night, wanting her so badly it hurt.

"I thought I would call Chance and see if he had some time today to show us some horses."

She nodded, looking at her coffee instead of his face. "Sounds like a good plan. And yeah, I'm all in. They have some of the best bloodlines in Texas. I'd be curious to see a few myself."

Seth took out his cell and noted the time: seven o'clock. Chance should be up by now. He pushed a button, and the phone began to ring.

"Seth? Hey, what's going on?" his brother answered.

"I'm looking for a horse. Do you have any that might be for sale?"

"For you? You bet. Why don't you come over about ten o'clock? Let me get a few things out of the way and I'll be glad to show you some."

"Sounds like a plan. Thanks, Chance."

"See ya later."


The Masters Ranch was immense. They drove past buildings containing offices, an on-site veterinary clinic and corrals and finally arrived at the main barn. The gabled building had enormous white columns set against green walls and a door large enough for cars and trailers to go inside. Next to the main barn door were smaller glass doors that opened into a lobby. Carpeted in dark green, there were several chairs and sofas. Across one wall was a display cabinet holding a slew of trophies. Down the hall to the right were offices. To the left and straight ahead were stalls, tack rooms and rooms for feed storage.

"This is unbelievable," Ally commented.

"It's big," Seth agreed. "The main structure was built before I was born. Over the years they added on as needed. Go straight down the main aisle and you'll find an indoor riding arena. Come on." He led her to an office several feet from the lobby. Chance was just getting off the phone. He looked up and immediately smiled.

Standing, Chance walked around his formidable desk and came toward them, his hand held out. Dressed in worn jeans and a long-sleeved shirt, he looked like your everyday cowboy.

"Seth, Ally," he said, shaking their hands. "Welcome."

"Thanks for doing this, Chance."

"It's my pleasure. So, what kind of horse are we looking for?"

Seth paused a minute. "I was thinking maybe a quarter horse."

"Good choice. We have quite a few you can choose from. Let's go take a look."

They followed Chance to a section of stalls just down from the indoor arena. Seth noticed Ally had become very quiet, but her eyes were alert and she seemed to be taking in her surroundings. She walked close to Seth, her hair gleaming under the neon lights.

"These are magnificent horses," she said.

"Thanks," Chance replied. "Most of our bloodlines go back quite a few years. My grandfather started breeding our quarter horses before I was born. He took real pride in the results eventually produced. Seth, I want to show you a couple that have been trained to ride but as yet haven't gone through cutting training. These horses can turn on a dime, sometimes when you don't expect them to. You'll find yourself on the ground in a heartbeat."

"I appreciate that," Seth laughed. "My goal is purely pleasure and that means staying in the saddle. I've seen what these highly trained quarter horses can do."

Chance stopped in front of a stall on the left. Inside was a large bay quarter horse with four black socks and a white star on his face. His coat glistened under the fluorescent lighting. A truly magnificent animal. Chance grabbed the halter hanging on the door, quickly put it on the horse and led him outside the stall into the wide hallway.

"This is Cajun's Creed. He's sixteen hands tall and smooth to ride, a quality not always found in quarter horses. He handles real nice. Would you like me to throw a saddle on him?"

"That would be great."

Chance led the horse down the hall, stopping in front of a tack room. Soon Cajun was saddled and ready to go.

"Let's go to the indoor arena. It's kept partially opened this time of year, and it's the closest. Here ya go."

Chance handed Seth the reins, and they walked to the arena.

Seth swung up into the saddle with no problem.

The horse held perfectly still until Seth was seated and ready to go. After a few rounds in walk, trot and canter, Seth drew the horse up to the entrance.

"He's nice," Seth said. "Ally, what do you think?"

"Me?" She seemed surprised he would ask her opinion. "He's definitely a keeper."

"I think I agree."

They tried out three more horses and came back to the first one.

"So, Cajun is going to be your choice?" Chance asked as he lifted the saddle from the horse's back and placed it back in the tack room.

"I think he's perfect."

"Well, all right then. He'll be ready to go anytime you want to come and get him."

"Would tomorrow be okay?"

"That's fine. I'm supposed to go to Oklahoma City in the morning, but I'll let the section manager know you're coming to pick him up."

Seth shook his brother's hand, and together the three of them walked toward the front of the building. Seth helped Ally inside the truck and they were off.

"That horse is fantastic, Seth. You're going to have a lot of enjoyment riding him."

"I think so, too."

"We can go and pick him up any time tomorrow."

Seth smiled. "How about we go home and discuss it?"

"Home, huh?"

"Yeah. I want your full attention."

"My full attention? On what?"

"Me." He looked at her and grinned.

# Twelve

"I'm thinking of sending the security detail back to California," Seth said over breakfast a few days later. "It's been over three weeks, and nothing else has happened."

"I think that's a good idea," she replied. "Besides, I can handle the intruder myself if he comes back."

Seth's eyes twinkled as he struggled to contain a grin.

"I don't care what you think. I have a perfectly good baseball bat sitting in the closet begging to be swung. Hard," Ally argued.

"You're too feisty for your own good."

"Call it what you want, but I want a chance to confront this guy."

"And what if he has a gun?"

She shrugged. "So do you."

Seth shook his head. "What am I going to do with you, Mrs. Masters?"

She shrugged. She refused to be drawn into that conversation.

"So, how are you and Cajun getting along?"

"Good. He's a great horse. Thanks for letting him stay in your barn."

How could she have said no under the circumstances, even if she'd wanted to? The horse was not a problem and got along with her horses very well. That made it possible for him to go out to pasture with the others rather than being kept in a stall. She believed in pasturing horses whenever possible and felt sorry for any that were stalled for long periods of time.

Seth was a good rider and seemed to love his horse. Where Cajun was going to go when Seth returned to LA, she didn't know. They hadn't talked about it. Seth was welcome to leave him with her, but he might have other ideas.

"I spoke with Chance the other day, and he said we could bring our horses over and trail ride all we wanted. How about this afternoon?"

"I'm getting in two horses to train this weekend, so this afternoon or tomorrow would be great."

"All right then. Let's go after lunch. I have some calls I need to make, but I should be finished by lunchtime."

By one o'clock they'd put one of Ally's horses and Cajun in the trailer and were headed for the Masters compound. Passing through the north gate, they ventured into the largest section of the ranch. They followed an old cow trail that took them over hills, through trees and down into canyons, where they discovered a lake at the bottom.

"Can we stop?" Ally asked. "This is so beautiful."

"Sure. How about over there next to that gray boulder?"

"Perfect."

Stepping down from the saddle, Ally tied her horse to a small pine tree. Seth followed suit. Together they climbed to the summit of the large rock and found a flat spot to sit down. Ally could see the river below them as it cut its way through the flatlands that seemed to go on forever.

"This is great," she said. "I'm amazed at how far you can see."

"As boys we used to trail ride all through this area. At the time, we were about ten or twelve. We didn't notice the picturesque quality, we just wanted to see what was around the next bend or over the far hill. There are a lot of stories about outlaws who camped in this area after robbing a bank or the general store in Calico Springs. We found old trapper cabins, one supposedly used by Jesse James and his gang. Wade once found an old revolver up in the attic of one of the cabins. That was a day I don't think any of us will forget. As boys, we thought we'd struck gold." Seth laughed, and his chuckle sounded deep and sexy.

"For me it was searching for pieces of pottery and

spoils from the Civil War," Ally said. "I've found a pair of eyeglasses, a canteen and several tin cups. Knives, old razors used for shaving and once an old rifle that was inside the trunk of a tree. The soldier apparently set it down, leaning against the oak tree, and left it there. Over the years the tree grew around it. I can't imagine why anyone would leave their weapon like that. But it's still there. I didn't have the heart to cut it out."

"That's wild. So...we experienced many of the same things growing up."

"I guess we did. I never pictured you here, in the Texas countryside. You looked like a businessman from the city when we first met."

"I am a businessman from the city," he replied with a laugh.

"Speaking of life in the big city, how are things going with the research center?"

"The blueprints have been finalized. And the official groundbreaking is still on track for the month of June, which is when I return to California."

"I see." And she did. Apparently Seth was counting the days until he could return to LA. She was counting down, too, only not with the excitement he was apparently feeling. She was going to miss him.

She shook her head to clear the tears that welled in her eyes. Seth had gone from being an arrogant stranger to a trusted friend. More than that, a lover and partner, helping her over the bad bumps in her life and standing beside her through the rough times.

"I wish you could be there, Ally."

"You'll have so many things to oversee, you won't want me getting in the way."

"That's not true. You're always welcome. Anytime. We may have started off on the wrong foot, but I'm glad for the opportunity to get to know you."

Seth looked at her with a serious expression. She felt her heart speed up as a delicious heat began to envelop her. Slowly he lowered himself toward her. She closed her eyes as they kissed. His lips were moist and succulent, and she was unable to stop the desire that sprang to life inside her.

She felt him cup her face in his big hands, and she melted a little bit more. He adjusted his position and lay down on his back, pulling her on top of him. Her head rested in his hands, his knee separating her legs.

"I want you, Ally," he whispered against her mouth. One hand moved to cup her breast, and with a squeeze she knew she was lost to this man. She wanted him, right or wrong, here and now.

Her hands came up and over his wide shoulders as she kissed him back, silently giving him the answer he sought. There was no holding out. No foreplay. No teasing. It wasn't necessary, she was so hot for him. There was something about Seth that tore down all barriers. Her body succumbed to his touch, his rugged scent, to the sparkle in his brownish-gold eyes. His deep voice sent chills through her and left her hot and wanting.

He slid off her boots then found the zipper on her jeans and quickly slid it open. "Lift yourself up for me, Ally."

As she did he pulled her jeans and panties down her legs and off her feet. For a second the soft wind touched her, and she felt bare and open. Seth rubbed his hand against her bottom, and she felt her body grow warmer still. She pressed against his hand, and he answered her need, pushing first one finger then two into her. The blood rushed to her head, and she felt encompassed in a soft cocoon.

Seth adjusted his position until she was covering him, legs parted, and slowly he pushed inside. Ally struggled to accept him.

"Take me inside, Ally," he encouraged.

Again his words caused a heady sensation to capture her body. She was drowning in Seth's possession and loving each second. When he was all the way in, Seth sat up and perched Ally on his lap. He filled her, and she succumbed to the mind-blowing sensitivity of her body fused with his. Then Seth began to move. He held her hips as he lifted her up and down, making her shiver with reckless abandon. Far below she could hear the sound of running water as the river surged into the lake, creating a small waterfall.

Ally was lost in sensation. She looked down into Seth's eyes, and her heartbeat doubled. Her breathing became fast as she saw her passion reflected in his eyes. She threw her head back. His motions grew faster and faster. She knew she was on the brink. Suddenly the dam broke, and she felt herself suspended between earth and sky, a thousand lights sparking around her.

As if sensing her climax, Seth wasn't far behind. He gripped her tight as he slammed into her, his hips lifting her off the ground. She heard him call out her name as he too reached his orgasm.

Ally fell forward, sprawling on top of him, momentarily too weak to sit up. He wrapped his arms around her and held her close, kissing her head and cheek. She heard his heart beating in his chest, his deep breathing as he strove to catch his breath. It had never been this way with anyone else. Not even close. But she wouldn't give in to her emotions and end up heartbroken when he went away. Seth had made it clear from the beginning that he was not a family man. He wanted no part of a wife and children, instead choosing to live his life as he always had: as a carefree bachelor. Not pinned down by anything or anyone. And the time until he would return to LA was growing ever shorter.

She'd had a glimpse of his life and knew she could never be a part of it. Not only for the reasons that Seth didn't want her there, but it was so far removed from the life she had always known. It had been especially nice walking along the beach with Seth, but she could tell it was something he rarely did. What would they do together? He had his clique of friends, his work, his routine, and she didn't fit into any of it. If he ever did decide to marry for real, she had no doubt he'd choose a woman like those they'd met at the restaurant in Malibu. And she had a ranch to run. She couldn't do that from LA.

"Ally? You're quiet. Are you okay?"

Summoning all her resolve, she pushed up and smiled at him. She was lucky to have known such a man. "Yeah, I'm good."

"I think we should probably head back. It's getting late."

"Okay."

She rolled onto her back, grabbed her jeans and began to dress.

Seth knew something had changed in Ally. He could feel it in the air. He could sense it in Ally. It wasn't because they'd made love. It went deeper than that. It had started when they were talking about the research center and him returning to LA. It wasn't anything new, nothing he hadn't said before, but this time was different because he was talking about leaving Texas. Maybe permanently. His intention was to come back and visit both his brothers and Ally, but he hadn't reached the age of thirty-five without learning that the best intentions sometimes didn't pan out. He wanted to see her again. Hell, he didn't want to leave her to begin with. No matter how he tried to picture it, he couldn't imagine being in a long-distance relationship with Ally.

He'd been single for many years, not accountable to anyone or anything other than his business. Running his company and trying to get the research center started didn't leave any time for personal relationships. And with taking on the additional responsibilities of Masters International, his free time would be even more limited. Any thought of making this a steady relationship, let alone continuing the marriage, was ridiculous. That's just the way it was, and he'd better accept it. Ally understood. Why couldn't he get it through his head that this was one relationship that just would not work out?

Two of the Masterses' ranch hands were waiting for them when they approached the main barn. With smooth efficiency the horses were unsaddled and loaded into the trailer, and as the sun set beneath the horizon, they were on their way home.

"It was a good day," Ally said. Her delicate features were barely visible in the ambient glow of the dashboard lights.

He reached out and found her hand. "Yes, it was a very good day." He kissed the back of her hand.

"That ranch is everything I've always heard it would be. The farther you go on the land, the more beautiful it is."

"Don't sell your ranch short. The Rockin' H has merits all its own. It has two lakes, hills, and the pine and oak forest is beautiful. Plenty of rich, good pastureland. And, from what I've been told, some of the best horses in the county."

She smiled at him. "Yeah. You're right. But still, there is one particular spot on the Masters compound I will always think of fondly."

"Maybe we will just have to find a special place on the Rockin' H."

"Maybe."

All too soon they were turning into the long driveway of her ranch. Seth pulled around beside the barn, and together they unloaded the horses and put them in their stalls. One of their ranch hands walked in and offered to see that the horses were brushed down and fed. For once Ally didn't argue that she would do it herself. Maybe she was finally understanding and accepting that some things could be done for her. No matter where he went, regardless of what he did in life, he would make sure she always had the help she needed. Her days would soon be filled with training new horses and no telling what else. She needed to be able to delegate some of her responsibilities.

And his life would be in California. At least for the foreseeable future once he left Texas. It was fact, and he'd better stop daydreaming of Ally and get back to reality. She was such a temptation, and he wanted all of her he could have.

Today had been unexpected and amazing. Making love in the great outdoors had been a first for him. He'd never been with a woman who was so responsive, so perfectly in tune with his own needs and feelings. He knew when he left to return home, she would close the door she'd opened to him. He hated the very idea. But, he reminded himself, he never intended to be a family man, never wanted to be married. He liked the freedom his lifestyle allowed. Still, for the first time in his life, he was tempted to give a permanent relationship a try.

Ally went to the barn to check on her brood and found two new horses eating their oats.

"They were delivered this afternoon," said Stony, one of the cowboys. "Didn't know for sure where you wanted them, so we put them in a stall. They seem content."

"You did good," Seth commented, looking at the grin on Ally's face.

"Yes, you did. These guys weren't expected until tomorrow."

"That's what the owner said," Stony explained. "The one on the left is a two-year-old named Denim. The other is three, and they call him Scout. Mr. Deevers said you would know what to do with them."

Ally nodded. She opened the first stall door and approached the horse.

"Good boy," she cooed. She ran her hands over the smooth glistening coat, checked the legs and moved to the head, where she checked the teeth. "He looks good. We'll find out how good in the morning."

She left that stall and approached the other horse. This was the two-year-old that wasn't quite as willing to meet a strange human. Eventually Ally won him over and managed to do a cursory examination. "We're gonna have fun, aren't we, Denim." She patted his shoulder and eased out of the stall.

"Have a good evening, Stony," she said and walked toward the main barn door.

"You too, Mrs. Masters."

Seth was beside her as they returned to the house.

He wanted her again in the worst way, but it was her decision. At the top of the stairs, she said good night and he had no choice but to continue on to his room.

It was midnight, thirty minutes past the last time

he'd last checked the clock, when he heard a soft knock at the door. Before he could respond, the door opened and Ally stood in the doorway. Without pausing she padded softly to his bed and leaned over him. She lowered her head to his, her lips soft and warm as she kissed him. Seth responded immediately, his arms around her shoulders as he pulled her down beside him. Then he was kneeling over her, kissing her deeply, wanting her more than he rightfully should.

"Seth, I…"

"Shh," he told her as he put a finger against her moist lips. Then he kissed her again, and passion flared between them. He didn't know what had brought her here, and he didn't care what the future would bring. There was only now: this moment. Whatever this was between them demanded his full attention, and he would gladly give it. He tugged her T-shirt over her shoulders, and when she lay back against the pillow, her full breasts were there for him to love. Scooting down in the bed, he held them in his hands and gently squeezed as he put his mouth and teeth into action. As his tongue played with the rosy tips, first licking then sucking, she arched toward him, letting out a small moan.

He moved up her body to kiss her lips, hunger driving him on. He felt her fingers play in the hair at the back of his head. His body was hard now; he was ready to take her. He wanted to taste her in the worst way. Leaving her lips he kissed his way down her body to the apex of her thighs.

"Spread your legs for me, Ally," he told her in

a jagged voice. When she complied he thought he would lose it right then.

He moved to her most sensitive flesh, loving the taste and feel of her. She drew herself up, lifting her hips toward him, and he fed. Her breathing grew fast, and she clutched the back of his head, holding him to her.

"Seth," she moaned, and her body grew still. Then spasms rippled through her as she climaxed, her hips bucking under his mouth.

When her tension began to ease, he moved slowly back to kiss her face. His entire body was tense and hard. If he didn't get release soon, he would explode. Using his hand he positioned his erection against her opening and pushed inside. She raised her legs to take all of him, and he pushed deep.

She was tight, and she moaned as he entered. He stopped, allowing her body to accept him. When he felt her push against him, he began to move.

With others he'd always held back, but with Ally his restraint all but vanished. He felt wild, as though nature itself were consuming him. The rhythm grew more frantic, passion overtaking all other emotions. When she came, Seth couldn't hold out any longer. It went on and on until both of them collapsed back on the bed.

He fell to her side, not wanting to crush her. He held her close to him, their bodies fused in moisture and the need for contact. He left a trail of kisses down her neck, loving the taste of her.

Eventually Ally fell asleep. Seth pulled the covers over her and stared at the shadowy ceiling. She turned onto her left side, and Seth caressed her smooth back and shoulder. He didn't want to give her up. Just the idea of another man making love to her filled him with anger. So what in the hell was he going to do?

# Thirteen

Ally slipped out from between the covers, leaving Seth to sleep. Quietly she tiptoed from the room. Grabbing some clean clothes from her room, she headed to the shower. Seth's scent was on her skin, and she didn't want to wash it away. She hadn't wanted to get up but instead lay in the bed nestled next to him. What was wrong with her? She was close to falling in love with him, and she would pay for it one day if she weren't careful. A day not so far away.

She stepped into the shower and let the steam work its magic. Today she had two new horses to train. She would concentrate on them and try to forget last night—and yesterday afternoon—with Seth. Try to forget how caring he was, how he made her feel wanted and protected. She'd been on her own for over a year, and she'd done well enough. If her ranch hadn't been stolen from her, she would have done better. Still, she didn't need a man in her life, and that included Seth Masters. She would make herself believe that.

She dressed quickly and headed to the barn. She wanted to get an early start on the new horses. Placing the halter on the three-year-old, Ally led him out of the stall to the round pen and started him off in a trot. The horse obeyed her voice commands and went around the ring perfectly, not requiring a pull on the lunge line to control him. After a few times around, she pulled him up and turned him in the opposite direction. He went around the ring less willingly, stopping several times to try to turn around. Whoever provided his basic training had apparently let him get away with going the way he wanted. Not happening under Ally's watch. The horse had to learn to take and accept directions, and that included going to both the left and the right on a lounge line.

She became so intent on working with the colt, she didn't see Seth approach.

"It looks like you have him trained already," Seth said from behind her.

She pulled the horse to a halt, giving verbal commands to reinforce the training. "He's already had the basics. That's one step ahead for both of us."

Seth stood next to the pipe railing, a mug of coffee in one hand. He was dressed in well-worn jeans that hugged his trim physique and a pullover sweater. He looked devastatingly handsome. His golden-brown eyes sparkled, and his full lips were tantalizing. A wisp of hair, bleached by the sun, fell over his forehead. He was wearing a gold watch on his left wrist. And on his third finger, his gold wedding band.

"Did you send your security home?"

"Yeah, I did. I can have them back here in a couple of hours if need be."

"I think it will be fine. The break-in was probably a onetime thing. I doubt if the intruder will come back."

"We'll be ready for him if he tries again."

"You've got that right!"

Seth shook his head, a smile on his lips. "You know, one of these days you're going to get yourself in trouble with that attitude."

"Why, Mr. Masters, I don't know what you mean."

"Hey, folks," their ranch hand Thomas Thurman said as he approached the corral.

"Morning, Tom."

"Stony and one of the other hands finished a perimeter check on all the fencing. They found three tree limbs down on the fence that needed to be cut away and a gate on the far side that looks like it's been forced open. We're going to repair that and put new locks on it. It looks like tire prints going through the opening and heading in this direction. None of us has been that route. Thought you'd want to know."

Ally felt Seth stiffen. "We do. Thanks, Tom."

"You betcha. Say, is Pauline in? I'd like to say hello."

Ally smiled. She'd seen Pauline coming from the barn and Thomas visiting in the house on occasion. She'd wondered if something was up between them. "She's right inside. Go ahead."

He tipped his hat and walked to the back door.

"Isn't that sweet?" Ally couldn't help saying.

"Oh, absolutely. Sweet," Seth said, his eyes twinkling. "How much longer are you planning to work your new horses?"

"I'm about finished with this one for the day. Maybe three hours on Denim. Why?"

"I've got to make some calls. I'll probably be tied up for a few hours."

"Go ahead. I'll be perfectly fine."

As Seth winked and walked away, Ally's heart pounded in her chest. There was something about that man that called to her. She didn't need his touch for her to turn to mush inside, just a wink from those incredible brown eyes. And that grin. And his deep voice. With a sigh she turned back to the colt. It was time to keep her mind on the business at hand.

Three hours later Ally returned to the house. Pauline greeted her with a shy smile and a blush.

"Tom said you wouldn't mind him stopping in," she told Ally.

"Not at all. Are you two now a couple?"

"Oh, I don't know if I would say that, but we're going out Friday night." She beamed. "He sure is a handsome dude."

"Yes, he is. Well, I hope you have a good time."

"Thanks, Mrs. Masters. I put on a pot roast for dinner. I hope that's okay with you."

Ally nodded and smiled. "That sounds perfect."

"It should be ready about seven o'clock. I'm also making a batch of my grandmother's corn bread rolls. I hope you and Mr. Masters like them."

"I'm sure we will. And Pauline, call me Ally."

Pauline nodded enthusiastically. "Sure will. Thanks Mrs.—Ally."

Still smiling, Ally headed up stairs to find Seth. He was in his makeshift office, still on the phone. He had a file in front of him, and from what she could tell he was having an argument. He switched lines and talked to someone else then switched back. There would be no lunch for him today.

She returned to the kitchen and grabbed an apple. She wanted to talk with Ben Rucker and figured while she was in town she'd stop by the sheriff's office to see if anything new had surfaced regarding the break-in. Holding the apple between her teeth, she hopped inside the truck and backed out of the parking place.

Ben had someone in his office, but Ally decided to wait when his secretary assured her that he shouldn't be long. But two minutes soon turned into twenty, and Ally decided to come back another time. She'd only wanted to assure him her dispute with the Masters brothers had been resolved. She was now certain they hadn't taken her ranch. Seth might have already spoken to him, which was fine.

Her next stop was the county sheriff's office. The

LAUREN CANAN 183

officer who had come out to the ranch was not in, but she was assured they considered the case open even though nothing new had come to light. Thanking them, she next headed for the feed store to order grain for the new horses. The owner had left a list of what they were accustomed to. She never liked to switch their feed immediately. If she didn't like what they'd been given, she would change to another supplement slowly, over several weeks.

"I figured I would find you here eventually," said a voice behind her as she left the feed store.

"Wayne." The very last person she wanted to run into.

"How ya doing, sweetheart?" His smile of greeting had a cruel edge to it.

Ally brushed past him and headed for her truck. She had nothing to say to this man.

"Aw, come on. Don't be mad. I had to leave. I left a note." He was following her.

"I have nothing to say to you. I don't want to see you again. Leave me alone."

"That rich guy is gonna drop you. Then where will you be?"

Ally kept walking, refusing to be drawn into any kind of conversation with the man.

"Dammit, listen to me." He grabbed her arm, and she yanked it away, finally turning around to face him.

"Don't touch me," she spat out.

"Look, I'm sorry I left. I had some important things I needed to see to."

"No, you didn't. You snuck out of the house in the middle of the night. But you know what? It's in the past. Leaving was the best thing you could have done for me. I'm glad you left. Don't bother me again." She continued to walk toward her truck.

"What about what we had? You and me?"

She ignored him and unlocked the truck.

"Did you hear me?"

"Save your bull for someone else. Whatever you think you left behind has long since died out. Now back off and leave me alone."

She got into the truck and tried to slam the door, but Wayne grabbed the handle and refused to let go. "You're going to give me what I want, sweetheart. You can make it easy on yourself, or we can do this the hard way."

Ally turned to him and glared. "There's nothing between us, Wayne. I want nothing from you. And there is nothing I have to give. Release the door or I'll call the police."

"Aw, baby, can't we at least be friends?"

"Stay away from me."

His cold stare should have frightened her but instead served to make her furious. She grabbed her phone from her purse and quickly dialed 911.

"You bitch," he snarled. "You haven't seen the last of me. You can try hiding behind that rich bastard, but if you do, just remember accidents happen. Either way, you're mine." He slammed the door shut and walked off.

"Nine one one, what's your emergency?"

"I'm sorry, I called by mistake," Ally said, locking her doors.

After another five minutes of assuring the operator there was no longer an emergency, she terminated the call and dropped the phone back in her purse. She put the truck in Reverse and backed out of her parking spot. She drove straight home, not bothering to stop back by Ben Rucker's office.

The encounter with Wayne had taken her by surprise and left her more than a little shaken. She tried to shrug it off on her way back to the ranch but hadn't completely stopped shaking from pure rage by the time she pulled into the driveway.

She remembered how Wayne used to love to fight. Had he been serious when he threatened to do harm to Seth? She couldn't let that happen. Seth was a different kind of person. Refined. Intelligent. He fought with words, not his fists. And while Seth might carry a gun, Wayne was a crack shot.

He'd changed since he left over a year ago. His actions and crazy talk reminded her of someone who was afraid of something. She knew behind all that bravado there lurked a coward. What she'd ever seen in that man she would never know.

There was only one person who could tell her what was really going on: her neighbor, Sam Shepherd. He'd been Wayne's friend for the two years Wayne had lived here. Without considering her actions, she backed out of the driveway and turned to the north and the Big Spur Ranch. She would find Sam. He would know what was going on.

She found him moving cattle on horseback. He closed the gate just as Ally drove up. He took off his cowboy hat and wiped his brow on his long-sleeved shirt, giving her a long, hard stare. He muttered something under his breath and walked toward her truck.

"Ally," he greeted her. "Long time no see. What's going on?"

"Wayne. Why is he here?" She got straight to the point. "What does he want?"

For a long moment, she didn't think Sam would say anything. He looked back over his herd like he was about to ignore her questions. But he didn't.

"Wayne's bad news. He's up to no good. You need to stay away from him, Ally. If he shows up at your house, don't answer the door. Call the police if you have to."

"Why?"

Sam spit tobacco off to the side. "Because he got himself into some trouble with the wrong sort, and he's running scared. I heard he's into them for some fifty grand. These are not people who extend payment terms. If he don't pay, they will take him out of the game permanently."

"What does he want with me?"

Again Sam hesitated. "He's looking for two gold and silver belt buckles he won at Nationals. He stashed them somewhere around your place. Figures they're worth a few thousand."

"There are no buckles at my house. I don't know anything about that."

If Wayne thought she had them, he was probably the one who'd broken into the house that night.

"I don't know what to tell you, Ally. If you don't have those buckles, he must think you already found them or you've got money. Or access to it. He was by here last week. Said you'd gotten married to one of the Masters brothers. He figured fifty grand would be nothing to you or your husband. Past that, I couldn't tell you what he's up to. I told him he'd better get ideas like that out of his damn head, but he just laughed and walked out. Haven't seen him since."

Sam spat again, and his eyes narrowed in serious contemplation. "You and your husband need to clear out of here for a while, Ally. Wayne's desperate. He got him a gun, and there's no telling what he'll try. He spent some time in prison for theft and found him a whole new set of friends. It changed him. That's all I know to tell you. You need to leave here for a while as soon as possible. The police have him on their radar but haven't found him yet."

Her first thoughts were of Seth. She had to convince him it was time to leave. Wayne was an arrogant man who could become mean with little coaxing. And he now had an agenda. Who knew when he would come back and try again? She brushed away the tears at the idea of Seth leaving, but he had to be safe. That was all that mattered.

She thanked Sam and turned her truck toward home. She couldn't let Seth be dragged into this situation. No matter how badly she wanted him to stay, she had to make him leave. She knew if any of Wayne's threats got back to Seth, Seth would not back down. She had to prevent that from happening.

Would Seth be hurt when she asked him to leave? Maybe. Or perhaps he wouldn't care. Would he ever come back? He had his brothers here. Maybe he would come back to see them but stay clear of her. Or would he walk in and want to pick up where he'd left off? Would he expect to be forever friends after what they'd shared? Probably not after she asked him to leave.

Her heart was beating hard in her chest. She needed to bring the police up to date. She turned her truck toward town and the county sheriff's office. When she got there, she explained who she was and what she wanted. The deputy who came to the front counter was aware of the break-in at her ranch and quickly put two and two together. He confirmed there was a warrant out for Wayne's arrest but no one had seen him as yet. Ally was asked what felt like a hundred questions but nothing seemed to help. The deputy finally urged her to return home assuring her they would put extra patrols in her area.

This was a nightmare. It was making an already bad situation into something much, much worse. It was already going to be hard to say goodbye, only now she had to find a way to make Seth leave to try to save his life.

As soon as she walked through the front door, she could hear Seth upstairs talking on the phone. From the sound of his voice, he was not happy with something the person on the other end was saying. Then his voice dropped low and she couldn't understand his words, but clearly he was talking about the research center project.

She went into the kitchen, stopped to grab a soda and made her way out the door to the barn. She'd let her guard down with Seth. She'd fallen in love with him. She knew that now. And now she was about to pay for it. Wayne returning only made the situation worse. Time and events changed a person. Wayne proved that. Once Seth was gone, would they ever see each other again? Probably not. She crossed her fingers that the police would capture Wayne before anyone was hurt. Especially Seth.

And Wayne… She wasn't sure how seriously he took her demands that he leave her alone, but he'd better figure it out. She didn't handle threats well, and Wayne had clearly threatened her this afternoon. Worse, he'd threatened Seth. She had nothing of Wayne's and she wanted nothing from him. She wasn't afraid of him. Maybe she should be, but she wasn't. What could he take? Only one thing made any sense: Seth really had to leave.

Entering the barn, she grabbed a brush and unlocked Denim's stall, closing the gate behind her. She'd forgotten to bring carrots, but he stood still for her as she began to brush his shiny coat. As much as she'd told herself not to fall in love with Seth Masters, she'd done exactly that. He must never know. He would soon be off on his next adventure as if nothing between them had ever happened, and that's the way it had to be. And once again she would be left to pick up the pieces of a broken heart.

Seth found Ally out back working one of the horses in the circle arena. If she saw him, she gave no sign. He approached the fence and stood watching her. Finally she pulled the colt to a stop and gathered the lunge line.

"Pauline left something that smells great on the stove. Are you about ready to eat?"

"No. You go ahead." She didn't turn to face him.

"I'll wait for you. It's only six o'clock on the West Coast. I still have some calls I can make."

She didn't respond as she ran her hand over the silky neck of the horse.

Something was clearly wrong. He didn't have a guess what it could be. He was due to leave in a couple of weeks, but they hadn't talked about it. He wanted to come back and see her every opportunity he got. Maybe that's what she didn't want.

He returned to the house and went straight to his office. He sat down in his desk chair and stared blindly out the window. They needed to talk. Their temporary situation had turned out a lot differently than he'd ever thought it would. He hadn't expected to grow so close to her. Have feelings for her that were a lot more than friendship.

Still, what could he offer her? He didn't believe in marriage—or at least real marriage. He'd come close one time. He'd even proposed, only to discover his fiancée was seeing another man and together they were plotting to get the money he'd worked hard his whole life for. It had been a close call. Too close. And he'd vowed right then never to trust a woman. Never get married. Never have kids, because kids were the ones hurt by it all. He knew that firsthand, too. He'd been raised by a single mother who loved a man who wouldn't marry her. He hadn't seen his father very often growing up. There was no love. There was no affection. There was money if they needed it, but that was all his father ever offered until the day he died.

Not that he believed Ally was like the women he dated back in California. Or like the woman he'd almost married. Ally was as honest as they came. He believed she had every intention of paying him back for the small amount he'd spent on furniture and lumber for the barn. At least she would try, but he wouldn't accept the money, because it was a gift. She had never given any indication she expected any more from him. She understood from the beginning that this was a marriage of convenience, and she knew it was drawing close to the time for him to go.

Suddenly he wasn't hungry. He would wait for her to come back to the house and they would talk. If she was ready for him to leave, he could go immediately, as if business required it. When the time was up, she could file for the divorce and it would be over. He planned to be generous and leave her a healthy trust fund to ensure her future would be good. He was determined she would never want for anything. It was the least he could do.

It was almost ten o'clock when he heard the back

door slam. It had to be Ally. He finished his call and hurried down the stairs. She was there, drinking a glass of water.

"Looks like we will need to warm the stew," he said. "The rolls as well."

"You go ahead. I'm not really hungry."

"Ally, what's wrong? You know you can talk to me."

"I don't need to talk to anybody. And nothing is wrong. Good night."

She brushed past him, and he listened to her footsteps as she headed upstairs. *What in the hell is going on?* He released a sigh. He would give her the night to cool off and maybe she would talk with him tomorrow. He hoped it was nothing he'd done. He hoped it was not about him leaving.

Because he had no choice.


Seth awoke the next day to find Ally already gone. Pauline didn't know where she was, just that she'd said she had some errands to run and would be back later. He pulled out his cell and speed-dialed her number. No answer. He hung up without leaving a message, not sure what to say. He poured a mug of coffee and sat down at the kitchen table. This was getting stranger and stranger. First she had seemed angry last night and wouldn't talk to him, and now this morning she was gone, no one knew where, and wouldn't answer her phone.

The house phone rang, and Pauline answered it.

"Mr. Masters," she said. "It's the feed store in town. They're calling for Mrs. Masters."

"I'll take it." Seth stood and walked over to where the phone hung on the wall.

"This is Seth Masters. Ally isn't here right now. Can I help you?"

"Ally was in the store late yesterday," said the shop employee. "She placed an order then left before we could get it to the truck. I need to know what she wanted us to do with it."

"Grain?" Seth asked.

"Yes, sir. Ten bags."

"I'll be there in a few minutes and pick it up. Thanks for calling."

Seth hung up the phone and poured the remains of his coffee in the sink. "I guess you heard, Pauline? I'm going to the feed store. If Ally gets back, tell her to please wait here for me."

Once he got to the store, the grain was loaded in the back of his truck in no time. Ally still hadn't been there. The owner said it was strange the way she left after ordering the feed.

"There was a man standing near the truck. I saw them talking. Then she got in her truck and drove off."

"Do you know who it was?"

"He looked vaguely familiar. If I had to give a name, I would swear it was Wayne Burris, but he's been gone a while now. Ally looked upset. If it was Wayne, I can understand why. He's no good."

# Fourteen

Seth got back in his truck. Why would she have been talking to Burris? Did they go somewhere together? Did they arrange to meet someplace? He didn't have a clue where to look. He turned the truck toward the Masters Ranch. Maybe she'd gone over there to talk with Chance about his breeding program. It was a far-fetched idea, but the only one he had.

Ally wasn't there. Chance hadn't seen her since the day Seth had picked his horse. Chance's daughter had been sick for the past week, and he'd been preoccupied with taking care of her.

Seth thanked him and started back toward Ally's ranch. Should he be worried? Could something have happened to her? He recalled the break-in. Surely that had nothing to do with Ally going missing.

He tried once again to call her. Still no answer. He drove around the area hoping to catch a glimpse of her truck. Finally out of options, he headed for the ranch house.

As he pulled up, he immediately spotted her truck. She was standing in the yard. He jumped out of his truck, slamming the door behind him, and rushed over to her with long, angry strides.

"Where in the hell have you been? I've been looking for you all day. Are you okay?"

"I'm fine."

"Want to tell me where you've been?"

"Not really." She shrugged. "Visiting some friends."

"Why didn't you answer your phone?"

"Didn't feel like it."

"Look, Ally, if I've done something to offend you…"

"No. You haven't. I just feel as though I've been wasting the past few weeks and I need to get back to business. People to see. Things to do."

"If this is your way of telling me to leave, just come right out and say it. I'm a big boy. I think I can take it."

"Any time you want to go…just leave. You've only got a few weeks left anyway."

Seth watched her and nodded his head. He'd been right. The impending deadline was looming, and this was obviously her way of getting it over with.

Maybe she'd made up with her ex-boyfriend, which didn't sit well at all.

"Fine. I had hoped we would separate on better terms, but okay. If this is what you want, give me a couple of hours and I'll be out of your hair."

Ally chose to remain silent. Finally Seth turned and went upstairs, where he pulled his suitcase from the closet and began packing. She was afraid. He could see it in her eyes. Was his leaving making her this way? He'd promised her he would come back. And he'd intended to try.

Why worry about it now? She was effectively throwing him out of her home with the least amount of effort. So he would leave. What else could he do?

With a curse, he opened the bedroom door and went back downstairs. He found her in the kitchen, sitting in a chair and gazing out over the pastureland.

"I thought we had something between us," he said quietly. "I thought you shared my feelings. I care for you, Ally."

He thought he saw her shudder, but then she shook her hair back from her face and looked at him like she was already bored with this conversation.

"Ah, but caring doesn't win the big prize, does it? I've realized I don't want to settle for a few romps in the hay. I want it all. Failing that, you might as well leave so I can get on with my life. Frankly, you're holding me back. But don't worry about the marriage thing. I'll still uphold my end of the bargain. Just file for divorce when the appropriate time has passed and I'll agree to whatever."

Her words hit him like a brick in the face. Something was going on. This wasn't like Ally. He stared at her trying to see a glimpse of the Ally he knew. Nothing. This Ally was cold, indifferent, calculating and appeared completely resolute in what she was saying.

He nodded. "Well, you certainly cleared that up. I'll leave tonight." He went back upstairs to resume his packing.

An hour later he was headed for the small municipal airport to board his flight home. There had been no sign of Ally when he walked out the door for the last time. He would have Karen call her to make arrangements for his horse. Maybe Chance would take Cajun for a while until he'd had an opportunity to work this through.

He was gone. Seth Masters, who had come into her life so suddenly, had left just as fast. There had been no goodbye kisses or hugs. How could there be when she'd thrown him out? But he was gone. That was the important thing. He'd gone back to California, where thugs like Wayne couldn't touch him. Seth would be safe, walking on his beach, working with his friends, maybe even dating some woman who was clearly on his social level. He would be safe and happy. That's all that mattered. Still, the pain deep inside wouldn't leave.

She gazed out over the pastureland. She owed him so much. She wouldn't have her ranch were it not for him. He'd given her reason to smile again. She couldn't help but recall those moments she'd spent in his arms. She'd felt loved and protected and so cherished. No doubt he made every woman feel that way. She was nothing special. At least not to Seth, who could have about any woman he wanted. The real kicker was, he didn't want any. At least not on a permanent basis.

She walked over to Seth's horse. Cajun nickered softly. She opened the stall door and approached him. What would become of Cajun? Seth would probably arrange for Chance to pick him up. She smoothed her hand over the horse's shiny coat and put her arms around his neck. Suddenly the tears she'd held back wouldn't be held any longer. She held on to the horse as the sobs racked her body. She loved Seth so much. She'd gone and done what she'd pledged not to do. She'd fallen in love with Seth Masters. This was not like the love she thought she'd had for Wayne. This love was real. It was deep and pure and all-consuming. And she was going to hurt for a very long time.

When her sobs began to subside, she patted Cajun and exited the stall.

The house was quiet when she stepped into the kitchen. She poured a glass of water, wishing it was something stronger. Her mind drifted to Sam and what he had said about Wayne and those two belt buckles.

She looked around the kitchen. They had combed the house and found nothing like that. Her eyes came to rest on the fireplace on the south wall. Ally walked over to it and looked up into the chimney. Nothing to be seen but black soot. When she reached up and touched it, soot began to fall down on the hearth. Could something be hidden in the chimney? It was one place they hadn't looked. She stretched, moving her hand deeper inside the chimney. Suddenly her fingers encountered a piece of fabric. It felt like some kind of bag. Her heart began to race as she nudged it from its resting place. Then it was free and in her hand. She quickly untied the small bag. Inside were two shiny gold and silver buckles. Wayne's. It was Wayne who had broken into the house. And he would be back for them.

If she knew how to reach him, she would call and tell him to come and get them. But no one knew where he was. She didn't have his phone number. Sam. Sam might know. She grabbed her purse and fished out the phone. She was relieved when Sam answered on the first ring.

"Sam, this is Ally. I found Wayne's belt buckles. Do you know how to reach him?"

"No. I don't. I haven't seen him again since we spoke yesterday."

"Well, if you do run into him, tell him I found them and he can come and get them."

"Ally, you don't want him in your house. The man is deranged. Take them to the sheriff's office and let them handle it."

Why didn't she think of that? "Okay."

She thanked Sam and headed for the truck, buckles in tow. She made it to the sheriff's office in record time and asked for Mason Crawley, the deputy sheriff who had come out to the house the night of the break-in. Luckily he was in.

Ally explained the situation, including the recent confrontation with Wayne Burris. The deputy came to the same conclusion that it was possibly Wayne who broke into the house. The deputy took possession of the buckles and advised her to not have any contact with Wayne if at all possible. He also issued a caution to not let the man in the house and to call 911 immediately if he showed up.

Ally left the office feeling somewhat better about the entire situation. But—Wayne was still here in Calico Springs and Seth was gone. How could that be anything but bad? Tears welled in her eyes at the thought that she could have had a few more weeks with Seth were it not for Wayne. But Seth was safe, and that's what mattered the most.

Seth sat in the private aircraft and stared blankly at the clouds that passed below. He couldn't get it out of his head that something wasn't right. It just wasn't Ally's way to come off like a gold digger, like a woman who needed him out of the way so she could find someone else. Someone wealthier. Dammit, he couldn't figure it out, but something had happened. And he had a feeling it wasn't good.

She'd been seen talking to Wayne Burris, someone she professed to hate. Ally was very strong in her convictions, and she wouldn't have been talking to him through any choice of her own. And she wouldn't have gone from making love to Seth, letting her emotions and her love for him show freely, to abruptly telling him to leave the way she had. The entire thing just didn't make any sense.

His cell started to ring, and he fished it out of his pocket. He didn't recognize the number.

"Hello?"

"Mr. Masters?"

"Yes."

"We have a bad connection. I apologize."

He obviously didn't know Seth was at twenty thousand feet in the air.

"This is Deputy Crawley with the Calico Springs County Sheriff's Department. I wanted to give you an update on the break-in. Thanks to your wife, as you probably know, we think our man is Wayne Burris. He was after two gold and silver rodeo belt buckles he'd hidden in the kitchen chimney. Mrs. Masters found them and brought them in this afternoon. She told us Wayne had approached her a couple of times trying to gain admission into the house. We know about the threats on your life. We have a warrant out for his arrest, but no sign of him yet. He's also wanted for grand theft in another county. It's good that you and your wife are leaving town for a few days. We spoke at length to your neighbor Sam Shepherd, and he confirmed Wayne has acquired a gun. Wayne Burris is out of prison on probation, and that's a violation. He's considered armed and dangerous."

"Wait, Deputy Crawley. Ally isn't with me. She's still at the house."

A knot of fear like he'd never experienced before tightened in Seth's gut. Suddenly Ally's actions before he left all made sense. She was trying to get him out of the house if Wayne Burris should come back. For God's sake, she was trying to protect him.

"Mr. Masters, we're in our final approach. Landing estimated in five minutes," the captain said over the intercom.

"Is there anything else, Deputy Crawley?" Seth said into the phone.

"No, sir. But I suggest you get Mrs. Masters to another location as soon as possible. We have every reason to believe Burris will go back to the house. I tried to reach her on her cell, but there was no answer. We have cars patrolling the area. But it's best to get her to a safe location as soon as possible."

Sweat broke out on Seth's brow. He thanked the deputy and terminated the call. Immediately he dialed Ally's number. No answer. He hung up and dialed again. No answer.

Seth unbuckled his seat belt and hurried to the cockpit.

"Gene, as soon as we land, be prepared to leave again. We'll be headed back to Texas as fast as this plane can go. I'm calling my security to meet us. As soon as they're aboard, we take off. Understood?"

"Yes, sir."

Back in his seat, Seth contacted his head of security and made arrangements for Frank and Bryan and one other staff member to meet him at the small regional airport as soon as possible.

He rubbed the back of his neck, just one thought circling over and over in his head.

*Please let us make it back to the ranch in time.*

Ally finished checking the locks on the windows both upstairs and down. The front and back doors were locked. With one last sigh, she turned off the lights in the kitchen and made her way into the den. Her baseball bat was next to the chair in the back corner. She pulled her phone from her jeans pocket, glancing to make sure it had reception. Just two bars, and the second was flickering. And there were five messages that apparently had not come through earlier due to the poor reception in the area. One from the sheriff's office. Four from Seth. She didn't have time to check them now. Placing the phone on the table next to the chair, she knelt down and waited.

She'd spotted the police cruisers driving up and down the road in front of her house a couple of times. While somewhat reassuring, she knew Wayne, if he came tonight, would sneak in through the back. No one on the road would know anything was happening. She was as ready as she could be. Maybe when she told him that his buckles were with the sheriff and Seth was gone, he would finally give up and leave.

She didn't know for sure how long she sat there. The old pendulum clock ticked by the minutes ever so slowly. Suddenly she heard the knob to the kitchen door jiggle. That was followed by what sounded like kicks to the door. It could only be Wayne.

She picked up the bat and scampered behind the chair just as the kitchen door crashed open. She heard footsteps on the kitchen floor—followed by two voices. One was Wayne's. Someone was yelling at him to get out of the house. Wayne shouted a curse, and seconds later, a gunshot rang out. *Oh my God.* What was happening?

She grabbed her cell and quickly dialed 911.

"Nine-one-one. What is your emergency?"

"This is Ally Masters. Please tell Deputy Crawley that Wayne Burris is here. At my house. He's just broken in, and someone has been shot." Her voice wavered when she said the last sentence. *Please don't let it be Seth.*

"Ally! Where the hell are you?" Wayne shouted out through the stillness.

"He's coming for me," Ally desperately whispered into the phone. "Please hurry!"

She terminated the call, placed the phone on the floor and double-fisted the bat.

"I know you're in the house, darlin'." She could hear him kick over a piece of furniture in the other room.

"I don't want to hurt you, Ally. I just need my buckles and some money."

Ally heard him stop in front of the door to the den.

"Come on out. I won't hurt you."

Slowly she stood up from behind the chair, the bat held at her side.

"I found your belt buckles this afternoon. They are at the sheriff's office. Had you told me what you needed instead of making ugly threats, I would have given them to you."

Wayne cursed. "Never mind the buckles. Cash will do fine."

"I don't have any cash."

"Lady, you're married to one of the wealthiest men in the country. Don't even go there."

She swallowed hard. "Seth is gone. We…we had a fight. He's gone back to California and will file for divorce. I don't even know how to reach him. He said his attorneys will contact me."

"You're lying," he accused as he came into the room. Ally saw the gun in his hand through the ambient lighting of the back porch.

"Have you ever known me to lie?" she said, looking straight into his eyes. They were cold. Calculating.

That seemed to slow him down. She'd always been completely honest with Wayne. He knew that.

"Then you'll have to do. Your soon-to-be ex-husband will get to pay dearly for your safe return or it's on his hands. You're coming with me."

"Where?"

"Don't worry about it. Come on. The cops will be here soon."

"I'm not going anywhere with you. I told you before, leave me alone!"

"Dammit, Ally. You always did have to do things the hard way."

He stuffed his revolver into the back of his pants and came for her. When he bent over to move the chair, Ally brought the bat into play. One hard *thunk* with all her might against the side of his head and he went down hard. He was moaning, and she knew she hadn't knocked him out completely. She had to get out. She quickly stepped around the chair, pulled his gun from out of his pants and ran for the kitchen.

Just as she threw the gun out into the darkness as hard as she could, someone grabbed her. She felt a very strong arm circle her waist and a large hand over her mouth. She cried out and fought for all she was worth.

"Ally. Ally," a voice said in her ear. "It's me, Seth. You're all right."

Breathing hard, she ceased her struggles. He removed his hand from her mouth as three large men hurried past them and into the house, guns drawn. "Seth?"

"It's all right, Ally. You're fine. We're both fine."

In the distance she heard the sound of sirens. She turned into Seth's arms and couldn't get close enough to the man she loved. The tears flowed as he held her. She couldn't stop trembling. His hand cupped the back of her head as he pulled her close.

"You silly woman," he said softly. "Sometime you're going to explain to me what in the hell you thought you were doing trying to take on somebody like Burris by yourself."

"He...this...it had nothing to do with you. It was my own bad judgment to become involved with him in the first place. I... I thought I could talk to him, make him see he needed to leave us alone and—"

Just then, Wayne Burris stumbled out the back door, in handcuffs, escorted by Seth's security team. The sirens screamed from the front of the house. Doors slammed, and the sheriff's deputies hurried to take control of the prisoner.

"Mrs. Masters, are you all right?" asked Deputy Crawley.

"Yes," she said, as Seth still held her close. "But I heard a shot. I'm afraid one of the ranch hands may have been hurt."

"You two go toward the barn and check to make sure no one was hurt," the deputy told his officers. They soon returned to report that one of the cowboys had been shot in the arm and the ambulance was on the way.

"You both will need to come down and give a statement," he said, "but it can wait until the morning."

"We will be there," Seth answered. "Thanks, Deputy Crawley."

The officer tipped his hat and disappeared inside the house.

"What am I going to do with you?" Seth said against Ally's temple. She turned in his arms.

"Just hold me," she said, and Seth's arms came around her, holding her close.

# Fifteen

The police left with Wayne in the back seat of Deputy Crawley's car, throwing out threats to any and all. Then the ambulance with the wounded cowboy took off for the hospital. Throughout all this, Ally still stood with her arms around Seth. Every breath she felt him take was a small miracle. She loved him so much. She still couldn't believe he'd come all the way back here to save her.

"How about we go to a hotel tonight?" Seth asked. "Then, after we give our statements in the morning, we will head to California."

Ally was too emotionally exhausted to argue. But this was her home. Good or bad, it was where she needed to be. The house would need repairs, the cowboys deserved an explanation and she wouldn't leave until all was seen to. But for tonight, a hotel sounded like heaven.

"Let's go." She smiled up at Seth, and together they walked to his truck. His three security personnel would stay at the house in case Wayne had any associates.

When they arrived at the hotel, Seth went inside to secure a room then returned to help Ally out of the truck. The room was just like the first one they had shared before they were married. Once they were settled, Ally headed for the shower, and to her surprise, Seth followed her in.

"Hand me the shampoo," he said, standing behind her. He took the small bottle and began to wash her hair, massaging her scalp, then moving his hands down over her shoulders. Ally bent her head as Seth worked the tight muscles in her neck and shoulders. At some point he poured soap in his hands and began to lather her arms and back then reached around to her breasts. She leaned against him as he massaged lower, between her legs. Shivers shot through her body. She turned around and took the soap from him.

Pouring some in her hand, she began to lather his broad chest and arms. She turned him around and went to work on his back, loving the feel of his muscles as her hands slid over his hot skin. He turned toward her and guided her hands lower, to his erection. He was rock-hard. She rubbed the soap over his silken shaft, loving the feel of him.

Seth pulled her to him under the spray of the shower and rinsed the soap from her hair and body.

Ally stepped out, grabbing a towel while Seth finished washing himself off. Then he took her towel and helped her dry off.

Before she could say anything, his mouth came down over hers. He tasted of spice and pure raw male. His hands cupped her face, and the kiss grew from compassionate to intensely compelling. He shifted his body so his bare chest was against her breasts, his erection pushing against her belly. His arms came around her waist. He slid his hands up her rib cage and massaged her breasts before finally giving due attention to the tips with his hot mouth. She couldn't suppress a moan as her nipples hardened under his attention. She ran her arms up over his broad shoulders and raked her fingers through his thick, damp hair.

She tipped back her head, allowing him to push her mouth farther open, giving him full access. They were now in their own private world. She met the intensity of his kiss with passion of her own, her nipples tightening with desire as she arched toward him. Flashes of pure heat coursed through her lower abdomen as she pulled him close.

Seth scooped her into his arms and walked to the bed. With one tug he threw back the covers and placed her gently on the bed, following her down.

"I'm so angry with you," he whispered as his long, muscled leg covered hers. He kissed her neck, taking nips along the way to her breasts. "You did a very stupid thing." He placed his mouth over one breast and gently began to suck. With his hand he cupped her other breast and began to massage her.

"No, I didn't," she responded between kisses. "Removing you from a situation that had nothing to do with you and could have gotten you killed was not a stupid thing to do."

Seth moved so his body was fully on top of her, his erection finding the core of her desire.

"Trying to take on a violent felon single-handed was." His lips again took hers. "You're a wild lady, Ally Masters," he said against her lips. His voice was so deep and sexy.

She didn't want to talk any more. She wanted Seth. Every glorious inch of him. She wanted to love him and rejoice in the knowledge that he was here with her. Maybe not for much longer, but she wouldn't think about that now.

Then he pushed inside her and the world outside the sphere of magic that surrounded them ceased to exist.

The next morning, once they'd made their statements to the police, it was time to return to Ally's ranch and figure out what their next step would be. As they drove up to the house, they saw three of the ranch hands out front waiting for them to arrive. While Ally went inside to assess the damage from last night, Seth approached the group of men to see if there were any updates on the hand who'd been shot.

"It was just a flesh wound," Tom said. "He was

lucky. We found the gun Wayne used in the shooting and turned it over to the police."

"That's great news. I'd wager Wayne Burris is going back to prison for a long time. But I can't apologize enough that you had to become involved with this."

"Heck, no problem here. Had we known what was coming down, we might have been able to help. We're glad you and Mrs. Ally are okay."

"Thanks again, guys." Seth offered his hand to each one. "I'd better get to the house."

He found Ally in the kitchen, muttering over the broken back door. Then she started straightening the chairs Wayne had kicked over. Seth followed her into the den, where he helped her set up the chairs there.

He was still amazed that this tiny woman had taken on someone like Wayne Burris and gotten the better of him.

"The cowboys found the gun out by the barn. I assume you threw it out there?"

"I didn't want him to find it and use it on anyone else. I had the chance to grab it when he was knocked out, so I took it." She shrugged like it was no big deal. "Seth, all of this was my fault. I am so sorry I got you involved."

"It isn't your fault, Ally. How can you possibly say that?"

"Because it's true. I made the wrong decision to ever let Wayne into my life. Granted, I never intended to get you involved, but nonetheless, I did." She walked back to the kitchen. "This is going to require a new door. I'll call a friend of mine and see if he has time to pick one up at the hardware store." She stared at the opening. "I guess, now that things have settled, you'll be on your way back to California."

Seth didn't move. He didn't want to go back. He wanted to stay right here with Ally but she seemed to be pushing him away again. Was that what she wanted—for him to leave for good this time?

"Ally, I need to know if you want me to leave, like permanently. And I need to know why."

She drew in a deep breath and turned to him with tears in her eyes. "This is my world. Cows and cowboys. Horses, rodeos and people who talk funny. We don't do social events, wear evening gowns, or know the meaning of words like posh. We don't travel in jets or live in penthouses."

"Ally—"

"You would be bored. And embarrassed to present me to your friends. We are from two different cultures that weren't meant to mix. And if someday we had kids, what then? We just wouldn't work."

"I see your point," he said finally. "And I think it's a load of bull. I love you, Ally. I don't know what that means to you but it means a hell of a lot to me. We would work by taking it one step at a time. By fighting for what we want. By showing our determination to be together."

"You don't understand," she cried.

"I understand more than you know. I wish to hell you did." He paused and rubbed his forehead in frustration. "I guess I'd better head to the airport. Are you sure you're going to be okay?"

"I'll be fine. This door is the only thing that needs repair. Plus, I have two new horses in for training with more expected, so I'll stay busy." Her eyes welled with tears, and she quickly turned away.

"Ally, come with me."

"I can't." She brushed the tears from her eyes and faced him. "You have your world and I have mine. We knew from the beginning this marriage or whatever it was wouldn't last. It turned out well for both of us. I really do appreciate getting my ranch back, and I'm enormously happy for you. That research center will save a lot of lives. We both know we live in two different worlds. I'm not a socialite by any means, and while you're pretty good with a horse, you're a city dude. You always will be."

Seth pulled her into his arms and kissed her. He could taste the salt of her tears. Ally would never admit she was wrong about him. Their worlds weren't so different that they couldn't bridge the gap. She might trust him, but she would never tear down that wall. He slowly backed away. Her eyes were closed, her face raised to his. Her refined features had never looked more beautiful. One tear slipped down her cheek. He brushed it away with his thumb.

It was an impossible situation.

"Take care of yourself," he said.

"You too." She forced a smile.

Knowing there was nothing else to say, Seth turned away and walked toward the front door and the truck that waited outside. He pulled out onto the white rock road and turned toward the airport.

Less than a mile down the road, he stopped the truck. Dammit, he didn't want to leave. Specifically, he didn't want to leave Ally. He had been shown what it meant to have a wife that was honest and loyal. Being here these past few months with Ally, and getting to know his brothers and their wives and children, had shown him the truth about caring for someone and knowing they care for you. He was a part of something, a family, for the first time in his life, and he wanted it desperately. His work and all he'd accomplished in the past seemed insignificant in comparison. He'd always been a loner, never spending very much time in the same place, but suddenly, he needed a home and, even more, someone to share it. There was only one person who could make it happen. He had to make her listen. He had to convince her.

He turned the truck around and headed back to the ranch. When he hurried into the house, Ally was nowhere to be found. He raced for the barn. She was there, sitting on a bale of hay, crying.

"Hey, you're going to ruin that hay with all those tears."

Surprised, she took a deep breath and brushed the tears from her face as she stood from the bale.

"What are you doing here?" Her voice was hoarse.

"I live here. That is, if you'll let me."

Ally opened her mouth as if to say something but instead shook her head.

Seth approached her, placing his hands on her shoulders.

"Things that might have once seemed impossible can happen, Ally. I'm in love with you," he said, lifting one hand to stroke her hair from her face. "I didn't expect it to happen, but it did. I want you to marry me for real and have my babies and be with me the rest of my life. I don't care if it's here or in California or anywhere else in this world as long as you're there. You are my home. You are my world. If you'll give me a chance, I know we can make it work."

He stepped back and raised her face to his. "How about it? Are you up for a challenge?"

"Are you sure, Seth? Are you sure I'm what you want?"

"I've never been more sure of anything in my life."

Her tears began to roll down her face. "Then, yes," she whispered. "Oh, yes." He held her close while he kissed her, over and over, cupping her face, unable to get close enough.

"I love you, Seth Masters," she murmured against his fevered lips. Then she whispered, "Welcome home."

\* \* \* \* \*

# COMING NEXT MONTH FROM

## HARLEQUIN™ *Desire*

### Available June 4, 2019

HDCNM0519

# SPECIAL EXCERPT FROM

**HQN**™

*Beatrix Leighton has loved Gold Valley cowboy
Dane Parker from afar for years, and she's about to
discover that forbidden love might just be the sweetest...*

*Read on for a sneak preview of*
Unbroken Cowboy
*by* New York Times *and* USA TODAY
*bestselling author Maisey Yates.*

It was her first kiss. But that didn't matter.

It was Dane. That was all that mattered. That was all that really mattered.

Dane, the man she'd fantasized about a hundred times—maybe a thousand times—doing this very thing. But this was so much brighter and more vivid than a fantasy could ever be. Color and texture and taste. The rough whiskers on his face, the heat of his breath, the way those big, sure hands cupped her face as his lips moved slowly over hers.

She took a step and the shattered glass crunched beneath her feet, but she didn't care. She didn't care at all. She wanted to breathe in this moment for as long as she could, broken glass be damned. To exist just like this, with his lips against hers, for as long as she possibly could.

She leaned forward, wrapped her fingers around the fabric of his T-shirt and clung to him, holding them both steady, because she was afraid she might fall if she didn't.

Her knees were weak. Like in a book or a movie.

She hadn't known that kissing could really, literally, make your knees weak. Or that touching a man you wanted could make you feel like you were burning up, like you had a fever. Could make you feel hollow and restless and desperate for what came next...

Even if what came next scared her a little.

It was Dane.

She trusted Dane.

With her secrets. With her body.

Dane.

She breathed his name on a whispered sigh as she moved to take their kiss deeper, and found herself being set back, glass crunching beneath her feet yet again.

"I should go," he said, his voice rough.

"No!" The denial burst out of her, and she found herself reaching forward to grab his shirt again. "No," she said again, this time a little less crazy and desperate.

She didn't feel any less crazy and desperate.

"I have to go, Bea."

"You don't. You could stay."

The look he gave her burned her down to the soles of her feet. "I can't."

"If you're worried about… I didn't misunderstand. I mean I know that if you stayed we would…"

"Dammit, Bea," he bit out. "We can't. You know that."

"Why? I'm not stupid. I know you don't want… I don't want…" She stumbled over her words because it all seemed stupid. To say something as inane as she knew they wouldn't get married. Even saying it made her feel like a silly virgin.

She was a virgin. There wasn't really any glossing over that. But she didn't have to seem silly.

She did know, though. For all that everyone saw her as soft and naive, she wasn't. She'd carried a torch for Dane for a long time but she'd also realistically seen how marriage worked. Her brother was a cheater. Her mother was a cheater.

Her father was… She didn't even know.

That was the legacy of love and marriage in her family.

Truly, she didn't want any part of it.

Some companionship, though. Sex. She wanted that. With him. Why couldn't she have that? McKenna made it sound simple, and possible. And Bea wanted it.

*Don't miss*
Unbroken Cowboy *by Maisey Yates,*
*available May 2019 wherever Harlequin® books*
*and ebooks are sold.*

www.Harlequin.com

SPECIAL EXCERPT FROM

**H HARLEQUIN**

*Desire*

*Honorary Westmoreland Thurston "Mac" McRoy
delayed a romantic ranch vacation with his wife for too
long—she went without him! Now it will take all his
skills to rekindle their desire and win back his wife...*

*Read on for a sneak peek at*
His to Claim
*by* New York Times *bestselling author Brenda Jackson!*

Thurston McRoy, called Mac by all who knew him, still had
his arms around his mother's shoulders when he felt her tense
up. "Mom? You okay?" he asked, looking down at her.

When his parents glanced over at each other, that uneasy
feeling from earlier crept over him again. Not liking it, he
turned to go down the hall toward his bedroom when his father
reached out to stop him.

"Teri isn't here, Mac."

Mac turned back to his father. His mother had moved to
stand beside his dad.

"It's after two in the morning and tomorrow is a school day
for the girls. So where is she?"

His mother reached out and touched his arm. "She needed
to get away and she asked if we would come keep the girls."

Mac frowned. He knew his wife. She would not have gone
anywhere without their daughters. "What do you mean, she
needed to get away? Why?"

"She's the one who has to tell you that, Thurston. It's not
for us to say."

Mac drew in a deep breath, not understanding any of this. Because his parents were acting so secretive, he felt his confusion and anger escalating. "Fine. Where is she?"

It was his father who spoke. "She left three days ago for the Torchlight Dude Ranch."

Mac's frown deepened. "The Torchlight Dude Ranch? In Wyoming?"

"Yes."

"What the hell did she go there for?"

His father didn't say anything for a minute and then gave Mac an answer. "She said she always wanted to go back there."

Mac rubbed his hand across his face. Yes, Teri had always wanted to go back there, the place he'd taken her on their honeymoon, a little over ten years ago. And he'd always promised to take her back. But between his covert missions and their growing family, there had never been enough time. Teri, who'd been raised on a ranch in Texas, was a cowgirl at heart and had once dreamed of being on the rodeo circuit due to her roping and riding skills. She'd even represented the state of Texas as a rodeo queen years ago.

When they'd married, she had given it all up to travel around the world with her naval husband. She'd said she'd done so gladly. Why in the world would Teri leave their kids and go to a dude ranch by herself?

He knew the only person who could answer that question was Teri.

It was time to go find his wife.

His to Claim
*by* New York Times *bestselling author Brenda Jackson,*
*available June 2019 wherever*
*Harlequin® Desire books and ebooks are sold.*

www.Harlequin.com

Want to give in to temptation with
steamy tales of irresistible desire?

Check out **Harlequin® Presents®**,
**Harlequin® Desire** and
**Harlequin® Kimani™ Romance** books!

**New books available every month!**

**CONNECT WITH US AT:**

Facebook.com/groups/HarlequinConnection

 Facebook.com/HarlequinBooks

 Twitter.com/HarlequinBooks

 Instagram.com/HarlequinBooks

 Pinterest.com/HarlequinBooks

ReaderService.com

**ROMANCE WHEN
YOU NEED IT**